REALITY CRASH

The Infinite Possible Saga

Damion Linder

INFINITE POSSIBLE: Reality Crash Copyright © 2016 by
Damion Linder. All rights reserved. No part of this book may be
reproduced or transmitted in any form or by any means without
written permission from the author.

Dedicated to my wife Roxy, thanks for the feedback and editing on all the chapters, my daughters Emma, Isabella, and Genevieve, I want to thank you for all your love and support. To my brothers, Seneca, Jared, and Jerel, you all have inspired me in so many ways. To even be at this point is because I got to watch, and observe all of your potentials for greatness in life. Thank you for all your great input, I love you all. For my close friends, thank you for keeping me on my toes and being fans of my work. To my parents who took the time to read, and give me feedback, you all rock! Also, Thank you God for everything and more.

TABLE OF CONTENTS

Getting ready for graduation seemed like such a long time ago and now…… It's here. It felt like just another normal day at school; exams, college counselors getting fresh new minds ready to enter the work force, then there was trying to figure out how many grad parties there were going to be and how many could you attend within a twelve to sixteen-hour span (without killing your liver, and the remaining brain cells). There was a time where I wish I could have been normal. Just part of the masses that didn't know anything, well anything more than what was force fed to you through the media, or our educational system. I guess for me it was never in the cards to be that way. As far as I can remember there was always something off about the things I saw every day, most people just seem to walk along the road of life and never seemed to notice. I always thought that I was strange, and of course the people that I would talk to about this thought I was strange.

Things took a turn for the weird a few days ago when I received a package in the mail. There was no return address, but something piqued my curiosity, and like a kid at Christmas I tore the package open. My heart stopped for a moment, it was a journal. It was worn, weathered, and completely full of writings. A familiar feeling set in as I flipped through it, I noticed scientific jargon, algorithms, equations, theories, some made sense, and some were just, well I couldn't begin to tell you what they meant. There was one section, though titled "Infinite Possible". This chapter was about multiple universes, and the relation of frequencies between them. Hmm, "Planes of Existence", "Universal Stitching Aka Universal Compression", what the hell is this?

Wait!! The writing, I knew this handwriting, UNCLE JONATHAN!!!! He would never let go of his research and he always carried this around with him. He would never let it out of his sight, so why has this been delivered to me??? I thought to myself, "Uncle……. You became such a recluse for the past two years. I know that he was working on something big, and that's why the family saw less of him over these last couple of years." He even told me,

"I might be busy, pre-occupied with my latest research, and my assistant, but if you ever need help dealing with school projects let me know. I am so proud of you, keep up the good work!!"

After that I haven't seen nor heard from him since. It's strange that I would have this in my possession now.

[END PRELUDE – DELIVERY]

A few hours have passed now, and I don't know what to make of this at all. Normally when people are giving you their most prized possessions, it tends to make you think they are planning on doing something bad to themselves in the near future, but this cannot be the case with my uncle. Should I call my Dad, and see if he's heard anything from his brother? I don't want to worry anyone, but not doing anything isn't going to yield any answers either. I'll make the call.

I Grab my cell phone and call my Dad. "Hi, Dad?"

My Father answers with a surprised tone, "Hey, I didn't expect this, so what do I owe the pleasure of the only kid I am not paying his tuition for?"

"Dad, we have to talk. I am concerned about Uncle John."

My Dad's tone changes, "Oh, well you know how he is, just because you haven't heard from him in about two years doesn't mean he's dead, hahahahaha."

I said, "Dad, this is serious!! He sent me one of his research journals. I don't know what this means."

The atmosphere on the phone changes immediately. "Wait, what do you mean one of his journals?"

I excitedly said "Yeah, there was no return address, no note, just the journal. I was thinking that I would receive an email or a phone call from him, but nothing at all. It's been a few hours since I opened the package."

My Fathers tone changes, and calmly says "Okay, okay, we all know what a shut in your uncle can be, we also know that you, and your uncle were close. Maybe he's sending this to you instead of calling to just let you know he's alive."

I say, "Dad we have his home address right? Do we know anyone that would be able to check on him to see if he's there, or has been there within the last day or so?"

My Father said, "Yes, I will call the landlord of the house he lives in, and check in every other couple of days to see if he's been seen. If I can't get a hold of him, within a week, I will take a little trip to look for him myself. To be honest, I wasn't worried about it initially, but after talking like this, I want to make sure he's really alright, and hey, it's been a little while since we've gotten together anyway."

Calmly, I say, "Thanks Dad, if you do hear from him, can you ask him what this journal is for, and also not to do things that freak me out like this?"

My father says, "Sure son, no problem."

There is a moment of silence with a sense of relief that can be felt on both ends of the phone. The abrupt silence is immediately broken up as my father says, "So, wow graduation, huh? What are you going to do now? You know that you can always come home."

As the conversation went on, the talks lasted until the early morning. We discussed my future, where I was going to work after school was over, girl, or girls I was seeing. We talked about the events back at home, the house remodel. I don't think I've ever talked to my Father for that long on anything. Deep down I knew what it was. He was worried about his brother, probably even more so than I was.

Graduation day, and there is still no word from my uncle. I tried not to worry about it, I had to convince myself that he was okay, and he would just mysteriously show up like he always did when I was a kid.

After the final speech was read, and the final cap thrown touched down on the campus fairground, I was met by my overjoyed parents. The conversation is normal for the most part, with my parents saying that they are so proud of me, my Dad saying thank you for not having to pay for the tuition, the jokes about my room conversion into the man cave my Dad always wanted. The atmosphere was interrupted on the way back to my dorm room; I notice my exam proctor pointing at me with some people looking in my general direction.

The proctor yells out, "James, can you come here for a second?"

I turn and look at my parents, and say "Mom, Dad, here are my keys to the room, make yourself comfortable, I will be right behind you."

My father puts his hand on my shoulder and with a smirk on his face says, "Damn, I guess they found out you were cheating on all your exams, huh?"

"Dad, come on, really? I will see you upstairs in just a few minutes. Mom there are waters in the refrigerator, I will be right there okay?" I said.

My mother steps in front of my father, and says, "Honey leave your son alone. Now James, remember we're going to that steak house for dinner, and I don't want to eat any of that junk food that you consider food in your room".

"Yes ma'am. Okay, you two, I will be right there." I said.

I walk up to my proctor, and introduce myself to the group of suits surrounding him. "James it's a pleasure to meet you, and thank you for taking a moment to speak with us. I hope your parents are okay with this. My name is Steve Bentclay, and I along with my team represent a company called Parasol INC. We worked with your Uncle a few years back. He always talked about you in such a positive way, especially regarding science, and that you have a keen mind. We have been out of touch with him over the last few years, but this moment is about you, and my promise to him. We would like to offer you a paid internship to Parasol Inc.

The money is decent, and it will get you to meet the right people for future project funding should you choose to go that route."

I am left speechless for a moment, but quickly regain my senses, "YES! Absolutely Yes! Look before I lose my composure here, about my Uncle, can you tell me what he did for you all, or when the last time you were in communication with him was?" I ask.

Steve's face changes. He has a look of apprehension as he is about to say something, but before he speaks, he is approached by one of his associates, who whispers in his ear, and then Steve says, "I understand. Look, your Uncle worked on some classified things for us, and for that matter that is all I can say regarding his business with us. He was my friend, but he, well he can be a difficult man to stay in contact with, I'm sure you can relate to that. As for the last time we worked together, that would have been almost three years ago, give or take."

I think to myself, "Three years, even I've seen him since then. I guess they wouldn't have any other information on his whereabouts, but if I start working for them, it's possible I can get a few leads."

I say, "Steve, thank you, I look forward to working with your company."

We shake hands, and I immediately head upstairs to my room. I can't wait to tell Mom and Dad the good news, and also hopefully get Dad to check up on Uncle Jonathan without alerting Mom about the current situation with my Uncle. Dinner is going off without a hitch, and I know that Dad knows what to do amongst all the congratulations that were in order. Just for a moment I could enjoy this day for what it was, an opportunity, and a chance for some answers.

[CHAPTER ONE END – GRADUATION]

The following week, my Father had called the landlord of the house dozens of times, but was either brushed off, or never got a response. He flew down to see him. The landlord told him that my Uncle hadn't been there in months and that he hadn't paid rent for this month. They did go in to investigate; I guess to make sure no one was dead in there. The place was pretty much in order aside from a couple books fallen off a shelf, and a TV still in a box, my Father had told me that it looked like no one had been there in a while. My father also told me that he would cover the rent until they could find out anything else.

There was a missing person's report filed with the police. One whole year goes by, and not one answer as to where he is, or why I have this journal in my possession. I started the job as a paid intern at a company called Parasol INC. They're a major pharmaceutical group that does a lot of government research, and also provides a lot of assistance to trauma burn victims with special skin graphing techniques. Honestly their work is amazing. Looking at the patients before and after pictures, you would never be able to tell that they had ever gone through such horrible experiences. I think about my Uncle every day and I start to wonder if he's even alive. I try and talk to my father about this, but he's pretty tight lipped about the whole thing. I know he's worried, so I try my best not to bring him up in conversation. Tonight's phone conversation is no exception.

I say, "Dad, hey man, just checking to see how the old guy is doing."

My father says happily, "Well your Mother and I are just getting ready to go out on the town, we're going to celebrate."

I ask in wonder, "What's the occasion?"

My father squeals like a little school girl, at a boy band concert, "Our investments in the stock market went up ten times in value!!! I cashed out half, rolled out another quarter into our savings, and left the other quarter in the share."

"Oh my God, Dad, that's awesome!!!   What are you going to do now with your new found wealth?" I ask happily.

"Well, son, retire. I don't have to work anymore; I am finally free. Also, there is something your mother and I have been talking about. We know that you've been waiting to save up for a new car, and since we didn't have to pay for college, we at least now, would love to buy you a new car."

"Dad thanks, oh my God. Thank you!" I say thankfully.

"Okay, well your Mother and I may not be back at all tonight, but come over this weekend so we can pick out your new whip. It's whip right, that's what the kids are saying these days?" He said with an inflection.

"Dad, its car, most human beings still say car." I say.

"Okay, see you this weekend, bye" my father says.

I can't believe it; I'm getting a new car! For the first time in a long time I do not have to worry about anything. Perhaps this will be a change for the better.

Just like that, I got my new car, and with it my professional and social life began to take a positive upswing. With everything going on in my life now, I started to focus a bit more inward, and stopped worrying so much about my Uncle. I had noticed that my father was doing the same thing. A few months went by, and I decided that it was time to get some new furniture for my place. With my new car I am able to drive out and meet clients as a representative of Parasol INC, which made me an asset to the company, because of that I am hired on full time with a nice pay raise. Back at my place, I started on cleaning up. As I began pulling some items out of the closet, my Uncle's journal fell off the top of the shelf.

The funny thing is that I hadn't thought about my uncle that much lately, so I decide to open it up again, and try to make some sense of it. The further that I go into it, the more I cannot stop reading. Some of the information here made absolutely no sense. It was like the science, theories, and overall analysis is based in total science fiction, then again, I wasn't really into anything like my uncle was when it came to science. I must have stayed in the same spot all night, well, I know I did, I can see the sun starting to break the horizon line. I don't think I've ever focused that hard on anything ever. Knowing that I am not going to be in any shape to work today I will call out for the day. I figure I will go to sleep, and then actually get some new furniture. I wake up and turn to see what time it is… "DAMN IT, its 8pm!!" I shout.

Well, I should get something to eat. I get up, brush my teeth, shower, and get into some fresh clothes. I head down the street for some food. As I start my walk down the street I feel like I'm being followed, but it's probably me being overly hungry. I make it to Vinny's, and on the menu tonight, spaghetti with meatballs. After eating

I started my way home, and again, I feel like I am being followed. I decide to walk around the block one time just to be sure. Taking the few extra minutes to walk around gives me some time to think about my uncle, and why we can't find him. I'm lost in my own thoughts, so much so, that I forget totally about that feeling of being watched. I'm finally home, and there is someone there waiting outside the building.

She's pretty attractive, I wonder who she's waiting for. As I walk up to the door, I know she's looking at me, so I say, "Hi, are you looking for someone?", and then she says "James, right?"

Confused, I ask, "I'm sorry do I know you?"

"No, but I know your uncle" she says.

There's no question, she's here for my uncle's stuff. I look at her straight in the eyes and say, "Wow, upfront and to the point, you must be here for the journal then?"

She says "Humph, you're a quick one aren't you? Good then this won't take anytime, give me the journal, you have a normal life, and you can forget that you even saw me."

I give her a cold glare and say "I don't think so; I want to know a few things. One, where is my Uncle? Two, are you the assistant? Three, who sent me the journal? It's not just something that he would just hand over will-nilly?"

She looks at me then points over to the alley beside my complex. She walks off first, and I follow right behind. Now I am confused about the situation. Of all times, why now? It's seems the universe is conspiring against me. For once things were starting to feel normal, and this is happening. We make it to the alley. She continues to walk towards the other end of the ally, and as I step past the threshold of the alley, "Okay, I think that's far enough, you haven't tried anything funny yet, but I am not going to follow you any further until you tell me what the hell is going on."

She looks at me with a smile on her face, "Your uncle used to tell me stories about you. You were always the bright one, the little kid that would make him laugh when you acted like a pretend scientist, wearing his overcoat and glasses, but more importantly, he thought of you as his own, like the son he would never have, he trusted you. More-so than anything else he recognized you for your mind. He raved about you simply put."

I smiled a bit, and thought, "Wow, really, so cool. Uncle Jonathan, where are you? We miss you." I realize that I am stuck in a moment, and I need to reengage the current situation, so I look at her directly, and ask,

"Wait, where is he, is he alive, and what is so damn important about the journal?"

She begins to walk toward my direction, then looks at me with this glare and rushes at me. She grabs onto my shirt and throws me into the alley. I crash into the side of the dumpster; it feels like I just got hit by a truck. My eyes, I'm glossing over, I got to get up, she's coming, GET UP! She's got me again, got to break the hold; I strike her in the face with an elbow, her grip released, rotating, good I'm behind her, I got her waist, I have to drop her now! I got her!

"HAAAAAAAAAAAAAAA", I scream out. What the, why am I losing consciousness?

FLASHBACK
James:
Dadddddd are we at Uncle J's place yet?

Dad:
Don't worry James we'll be there in just a few more minutes. I'm starting to think you like going over to your Uncle's house more than your own home.

James:
Well, Mom won't let me blow anything up there.

Dad:
Hahahahahahaha, indeed son, you are correct. You know how your Mom is when it comes to keeping the house in one piece.

James:
Yeah, she's never any fun. Why did you ever marry someone like her?

Dad:
So we could have you, son

James:
Awwwwww, Dad, C'mon

"DAD!" I gasp for air, reaching out. What's going on, why am I lying on my couch?

"Finally awake, I see. If I had known you were able to fight in the slightest, I would have handled things a bit differently, and oh, by the way, my name is Jill."

"Why the hell did I pass out, and why are you following me?" I ask.

"It doesn't matter how I knocked you out, look the less you know anything about me the better, you understand?" Jill says.

"I don't understand; I don't know why you're not answering any of my questions. I am trying to keep my cool, and it's obvious that you think I am not in any position to bargain, but I assure you, you haven't been able to find the journal." I say with a growl.

"Wow bearing your fangs, when you don't know whether you are predator or prey. I assure you I would have torn, and torched this whole place to the ground to find it, but out of respect for your Uncle I haven't. I need to get it back, now" Jill says.

I ask, "At least tell me why you were following me, and don't tell me it was because you thought I was being followed."

"It was because I thought you were being followed. I had checked up on your parents."

Before Jill could get another word out, I shout "MY PARENTS?! JUST WHAT THE HELL IS GOING ON?! WHERE IS MY UNCLE?!"

Jill just looks at me and sighs, "Are you done yet? For one, this was your Uncle's request, and two, stop shouting."

She's right, what if someone had heard us. I need to collect my thoughts. I have to get some straight answers out of her, and fast. I look up, and decide to get the journal.

I say to her "Move, you're in the way."

She got this look on her face, "you're in no position to tell me what to do right now."

"Oh and you are? You're in my way; if you want the journal, then move!!" I say sternly.

Jill gets up and steps to the side.

Looking down the backside of the chair firmly pressed up against the wall I pull it forward and lean the chair forward to pull the journal from the under-inner side.

Jill laughs, "Really, the one place I didn't think to check, and I was sitting on it the whole time."

I just shake my head, and as I start to hand it over, the journal falls out of my hands. The journal opens to the back cover, and it seems that the last page is attached, or stuck to the back. Let me just peel this back… huh, a message?!

> *"A place in time that finds a moment of eternity shall see the future's past momentarily. What is viewed is nothing more than a dream of events for tomorrow."*

I turn the page to Jill and ask, "Hey, what's this all about?"

She smiles, and says "it's just the Ramblings of a mad man your uncle and I ran into a year ago. He was harmless enough, hahahahaha it was strange, I felt like I knew that old man, and with everything that your uncle and I went through, I just brushed off any type of notions like that."

I look down at the journal, and ask "Why is that?"

Jill said, "Like I said, the less you know about me the better. Now I've extended my stay here, please give me the journal." I hand her the journal.

"So, just one thing before you go, my uncle, is he alive?"

She starts to walk out of the door; she stops, looks back at me, and says "I don't know, we haven't talked in a few weeks. He's a hard man to find when he doesn't want to be found, but after everything that has happened I can't be certain. Like I said, the less you know about me, the better."

I sighed, and said "I know I can't ask anything else, however, if you find my uncle, regardless of his status, please inform me either way. At this point I can handle any type of news; I just hope he's okay."

Jill looks at me on her way out of the door, and she says, "It's a promise".

[END CHAPTER TWO - MEETING]

Jill walks outside, and I can't see where she's going to anymore. I have to make a decision, and now. My Uncle is in trouble, and if she was tailing both my parents and I, who was she watching out for? I have no idea how to handle what may be coming after her, or my uncle. Ah, I can't be so indecisive, it's time to find out what's really going on! I run outside in the direction that Jill is walking, 2 blocks, 3 blocks, 4 blocks, how the hell is she so fast? I didn't see her get into any vehicle, where is she?!

As I turn around I see some car lights in the distance coming towards me, FAST!! The high beams turn on, "THE HELL MAN?!" I scream as I move out of the car's way. I can hear the brakes squeal. "Damn, what's going on, " I'm thinking.

The lights on the car turn off, and the doors open up, I duck down behind the dumpster. Two females are talking, "Did you get him? Was that the one we were supposed to be following?"

The other woman responds, "Did it sound like we hit him? Does the car look like we hit him? Listen, I need you to think about these questions before you vocalize, understand Agent Decem? We're spending too much time talking, search the area, and see if he's hiding somewhere."

Agent Decem responds "Understood Agent Tres".

"Tres, and Decem, got it. Now how do I get out of here, they're getting close, and I can't move or I will be seen."

Agent Tres says, "Search to the end of the alley, he has to be here."

Decem makes it to the end of the alley. "Ma'am, I've lost sight of the target, I'm coming back".

I am able to crawl under the dumpster. She walks right by me. The engine begins to rev, I hear the doors close, the car pulls out, and I sit and wait for the sound of the car to disappear.   I know that I have to get back to the apartment. I'm cautious as I start to walk out of the alley, but something feels wrong, I'm not alone.

"The less I know about you, the better right?" I said.

"I'm not going to tell you to come with me, but you must know what they are looking for, and now that they've tried to physically come after you, they will not stop. It's your choice." Jill says.

"My parents will be alright won't they?" I ask.

"Look the agents haven't tried anything physical against them, so it's a good indication that they won't do anything, but that's not to say that they won't. Your Father and Uncle are brothers after all. If you want to protect them, and yourself, you are going to have to come with me. After tonight, no contact with anyone you know. Meet me here tomorrow night at the same time if you want to protect everyone you love or care about." Jill says

I can't help but to feel like I'm in between a rock and a hard place. I'm scared, not just scared, but terrified. What kind of world is actually out there? This feeling I'm having, feels like the blinders are coming off, and I'm about to see a whole bunch of ugliness. I guess all those conspiracy stories that you find on the internet are starting to sound like the truth a little. I've made up my mind, I will meet her tomorrow. I turn around thinking she would still be there, but something told me she was already gone. I wanted her to see the resolve in my eyes, but she will know tomorrow. I don't turn around, I just walk out of the alley and back to my apartment, possibly for the last time. I thought about my uncle.

FLASHBACK

Uncle Jonathan:
Remember, it's not about how you do something, but why you are doing it. There must be courage in your action, don't falter, and find a way to fly.

James:
Huh, what are you talking about Uncle J?

I remembered he just smiled at me after that. He didn't seem to have a care in the world at that moment, just a big light around him that day. That was one of the last times I really remember him smiling. I called up my parents to check in to see how they were doing, and how they were enjoying retirement. I talked to my parents for a couple of hours. I told my Mom I loved her, and she told me that she can't wait to see me, and my Father said he was proud of me. I guess ultimately I couldn't have asked for a better conversation, I felt loved and acknowledged by the people that meant the most to me.

The next day I called out for a family emergency from work, and told them I might be out for a few days. I called my friend to check in on my place from time to time. He asked me where I was going, and I simply said that there are some family issues of a serious nature that I have to take care of. Honestly, I have no idea if I'm ever coming back. What I'm giving up now, and what I find myself seeking will definitely redefine me as a person, there's no going back. I'm just going to sit here and watch the sun go down, and go meet Jill. Here and now, I'm terrified, excited, and overly anxious all at the same time. I have to bear down and focus, let me just enjoy the last day of the world I used to know, because tomorrow I'm sure I will see the real world for the first time.

[END CHAPTER THREE - DECISION]

Not to sound like every cliché statement made in adventure movies, or books, but it's a new dawn. This will be the first time I go through the rabbit hole, and see what the world is really like. My heart is racing; I can't believe I'm so on edge. I have to calm down. I would have thought after last night that I wouldn't be so worked up, but I am. I feel like I am going to explode, and I can't decide if it's because I'm terrified, or excited. Heh, maybe it's both. I'm hungry; I guess that's a constant that will never change. I go to the refrigerator to see what I can find.

There's a sound at the door, "**KNOCK, KNOCK!**"

I freak out a bit. Slowly I gain my composure, and say "Hello."

"James, it's me Travis. Are you naked?" Travis says sarcastically.

I open up the door quickly, "Dude get in here! What's up man? Thanks for coming over to take care of the place, but you're here early."

Travis looks down and says, "Yeah well my girl and I got into an argument. Something along the lines of her saying that she saw me with another girl".

"And did she see you with another girl?" I ask.

"Yeah, but it wasn't what she thought. We weren't doing anything I was just talking to her, having a conversation. Sure, I may have been flirting a bit, but there was no intent to do anything."

I just give him that raised eyebrow look, and said "Right."

He looks at me, and says "seriously bro? Whatever man, I guess it was just perfect timing. Look aside from that, do you need a lift to the airport, ummmm, where exactly are you going?"

I raise my hand up and shake my head, "Don't worry about it, I have transportation already taken care of. How about we have some breakfast?".

We talked for a while; it's good that he came over early. I told him that he could stay for as long as he wanted, and hopefully that he could work out things with his girlfriend. We said our goodbyes, and I headed out. There were still a couple hours left, and I couldn't think of a single thing to do but wait. I wasn't going to hang out by the alley for sure, so I decided that I was going to head out to the park near where I live. "I'll just wait there for the day to end." I thought.

Sitting here I feel calmer, and I think about everything that happened within the last couple of days. I think of my family; I think of the last conversation I had with them on the phone. I think about my Uncle, and why I am here getting ready to do God knows what. The sun is setting, and with that sets in the final confirmation that my world will now officially change.

The sun has set, and now there is no turning back. Any worries that I have about what is going to happen seem to just fall by the wayside. I have a mission, and honestly, I can't even believe I'm saying this to myself, "I have a mission".

All I can think about now is my Uncle; I just want to make sure he's okay. Even his assistant doesn't have tabs on him, and I could tell from last night she was worried. With all these feelings welling up inside of me, I decide that it's time to head to the alley, I just hope that I don't run into any more cars trying to run me over. LET'S GO!

The distance to the alley is closing in, and I can't tell if anyone is there, but I'm here now, and no one, did I just get played? I can hear a vehicle closing in, this time I bolt back around the other end of the alley. The car lights cast a shadow over everything in the alley, it's so bright. I have to pull my head back, and hope that either this ride is for me, or have enough time to realize that I have to get the hell out of here. I hear talking, the voices from last night, why are they back, were they tailing me from somewhere else? I need to get out of here, now!

As I turn Jill is right in my face. I can hear the two females getting closer to the edge of the alley, and if they see me I'm screwed. In that thought Jill grabs and slams me up against the building wall. "Oh no, I'm going to die! NO!" I thought. I've been setup!

"Decem, we're here for clues. Let's not waste time" Tres said.

As they crossed Jill pressed her face up against mine, "She's kissing me?!" Something's not right, but at this moment I get it, so I lock in and return the favor I will probably only get this once with her.

I hear Tres say "Pshh young love. Let's go Decem, this is a dead end. We will have to report to headquarters now."

Decem quickly responds, "Yes ma'am".

I notice the sound of the car fade into the distance. Jill pulls back, and I'm stuck in a stupor for just a moment.

She says, "You're an idiot you know that? How could you just come back, and almost get killed by a moment of freakishly timed coincidence?"

I step off the wall, take a few steps forward, and look back at her, "Sorry, but I thought you were going to be there."

She looks at me with a strange expression, and looks down for a second, "Well I'm here, and it looks like not a moment too soon. Let's go, before I change my mind. We've a long couple of days ahead, so I hope you've rested up."

"Wait before we go, can you tell me who these people were that were trying to hit me last night?" I ask.

Jill quickly responds, "Now is not the time, but just know you must do what I say when I say it.

These are not the type of people you want to mess with right now, so let's go!"

I look right at her, smiling. I know that I've set my path, and there is no turning back, and I say to her "Yes ma'am!"

She looked choked up for a second, "Don't call me ma'am, I am not your Mother, we just made out right here for God's sake!" she said in an irritated manner. "So, you like...", and before I could finish she blurts out

"SHUT UP LET'S GO!"

Throughout the night we walked. Nothing was said, as if I could really find the words to say anything at all right now. We make our way out of the city limits, and stop at a parking garage. We take the elevator to the top of the parking structure, and there's nothing here. I was expecting a car at the very least.

Jill turns and says, "How heavy is your pack?" "It's about 10 pounds, why?" I ask.

Jill points to a building in the distance. "We need to get to that building from here. It's the last place your uncle and I worked at together. We cannot get to it by foot due to the gating of the area, but it's not so secure that we cannot get to it by rooftop. Let's go, just follow my lead."

Jill begins to run and jumps across the next building, and continues on. She looks back at me, and I know I have to start moving now. Growing up as a kid we used to do hairball stuff like this, just not stretched across so many buildings. I take a deep breath and start to run. I know that I shouldn't look down, but I do. "WHOA!" I let out a yell. I can see Jill, and she is still going. "It's either now or never" I say to myself. I back up, and begin the run again. Faster, faster, faster, jump! I clear it with feet to spare, but before I can pat myself on the back I can barely see Jill. I start moving again, jump, another building, another building, and another. Now I wish I would have done Parkour training with my roommates back in college.

Jill turns in the distance with an impatient stare like she is mentally telling me to hurry up. A few minutes later I make it to the destination. It feels like my legs are going to fall off my body, and my lungs are on fire. Panting away Jill shakes her head, and says, "Look, if you're going to be tagging along with me, you need to be faster than that, but not bad for your first run. Follow me."

We walk past the rooftop access door, and walk around the side, and see an electrical junction box.

Jill says "Pay attention. When I say pull the switch here, I need for you to pull the lever to shut the power off. I still have a common access card for the facility, but I don't need anyone knowing that I'm here. The moment I swipe; you pull the switch so the log time won't be recorded. There is about a two second delay in the log recording. If we time this right, there should be no record of my entrance. With that, the cameras in the building should be off for about 5 minutes. That will give me enough time to get to the office where your uncle and I worked at, and pull the files on-site here."

I shrug my shoulders, and say "Well I've heard crazier, let's do this."

Jill begins to walk to the door, the sounds of her feet stop, I grab the lever, and I hear her say, "NOW!"

I flipped the switch, and the emergency lights turn on. I hear the door close. "Okay, she didn't say what to do once she left. Let me back away from here and take some cover." I thought. I stop to look at my watch. I imagine that she will be up here in 5 minutes. I will stay out of sight until then. For now, there is no other plan except to wait. No more than two minutes after the power outage the access door opens, and it's not Jill that comes out, it's building security. They have no weapons drawn, just flash lights, and walkie-talkies. I hear the guards identify themselves.

"This is Officer Diaz; we are on the rooftop now."

"This is Officer Miles, confirming the initial investigation of the rooftop access with Officer Diaz. We are now searching the area."

You can hear the acknowledgement from their communication office respond, "Copy that. Please update once the area has been investigated."

The guards walk the perimeter, and a minute later I hear, "Miles get over here! I found the cause of the outage. We got some prankster, free runner most likely pulling switches.

"Damn it!" says Diaz. "Communications this is officer Miles; the problem has been discovered. It seems to be someone has pulled the power switch here on the rooftop."

"This is communications, the issue has been noted, please stand by."

A few seconds go by, "Officers, the technician has informed us to go ahead and throw the switch and wait 5 minutes until the power is restored. Please monitor the light sequences. If anything other than green lights shows in the status indicators, please alert communications immediately."

"Great, well I guess we're stuck here for a few minutes Miles." Officer Diaz said.

"It's all good man. I don't hear anyone around, so we got a little break, no big deal. I will walk around the area, and make sure it's clear." Miles says.

I have to be careful not to make noise. If he gets close, I'll have to move. "Damn it, Jill better not to get caught coming out of here. For the time being the access door is not covered. Stay alert and be quiet." I think to myself. Luckily, Miles just seems to be taking a general look across the rooftop and not actively investigating the whole area in person.

"Two minutes until the power comes back on. We will be able to access the building once it's turned back on." Officer Miles bellows out. I can see Diaz's shadow in the distance thanks to the emergency lights.

"I can't believe that someone would flip the switch manually. These pranks aren't funny." Officer Diaz says.

Officer Miles replies, "Well, this type of switch can also pop If there is dirty power running through the system, but there is no way to tell how it happened. I have told HQ that we need a set of cameras up here at least around the generator area, and the access door. You would think that would be common sense."

"Yea, but they don't consider this building high enough on the priority list to invest in it entirely, even though they do some pretty cool things here. You're right, I mean there are a lot of government employees, and military walking through here that you would feel this building, and what goes on here, would be seen as important." Officer Diaz says.

"Well, it's neither here nor there, let's walk the perimeter and get back inside. The power should be on by the time we finish." Officer Miles says.

The two officers begin to walk the area, and it will just be a matter of time before they will search the area that I am at.

"Jill please, I need you to hurry up!!" I think to myself. Timing would be of the essence here. I just don't need any confrontation right now, I'm not sure how I would be able to handle myself against these guys, and I don't need Jill worrying about me in the process. For now, I just need not to get caught up here. I have to be ready to move if they get near. From my position I can see them walking around the bend, I don't want to move if I don't have to, but if they split up coming around the other end then I'm screwed. It's a long drop down, and I don't have wings.

I hear the two officers talking, which means they are still walking in tandem. Okay, just watch watch. I can feel the sweat running off my forehead, I'm getting tense, and I have to calm down.

"Miles, let's split up from here." Officer Diaz says.

"NO!" I thought. As they start their walk towards my direction, they're close! "No, no, no, no!" I'm screaming in my head. Just then the power turns back on, and they start to walk to the access door. First, I was relieved, but then I think, "Oh no, Jill!" My mind is racing a thousand miles a minute, "what do I do?"

At that moment I found a rock, I throw it as hard as I can at the exhaust funnels on the other side of the rooftop. Officers Diaz and Miles stop, and run to the location of the sound.

"Miles you see anything?" Diaz hollers out.

Miles responds, "Almost there, okay, nothing, there's nothing. Wait I see something. Oh man, it's a dead bird. It must have flown into the wall here. There's nothing else to report let's go back."

Miles yells out, "Roger that!"

The two officers head back to the access door. I hear the electronic swipe and the door open, and then close. There are no other sounds, it's quiet.

"Where is Jill?" I think. I start to walk to the access door. Now that I know there aren't any cameras I can make my way back to the access door with no issues.

Then out of nowhere "Hey", a voice whispered. It was Jill.

"Are you okay, you look like you've seen a ghost? I've never seen anyone jump so high, hahahahaha!" she said.

"You scared the crap out of me, you know. You have no idea what was going on up here?" I say nervously.

She looks at me with a raised eyebrow, and says "Oh what two security guards walking around closing onto your direction, you throw a rock to distract them when the power comes on thinking probably that I hadn't made it out of the building, nice move, by the way."

She seems to be amused, I wasn't, but now is not the time to be worried.

"Did you find what you were looking for?" I ask.

Jill pulls around a backpack that she must have acquired from inside the building. "Everything we need is in here. I was actually surprised that the office remained the way we left it. I grabbed the laptops that we used during our tenure here at this site. I just need to get them charged. Also, I have the files of where your Uncle worked, and possibly sites he is still contracted through. These clues should help us to find out where he is, and what's happening with him."

I feel relieved. I never thought we would get this kind of information so quickly, but that doesn't mean tracking him down is going to be as easy.

"Okay, so where do we go to do this?" I ask.

Jill says, "Let's go back to the parking garage; I have a vehicle at the 5th level. We'll take that to a location that I have in mind. You can unwind for a bit, and we can start combing through the Intel that I just gathered. A few buildings over there is a fire escape that we can take down to the ground level. It's a straight shot to the garage from there."

As we head back to the garage I think about my Uncle, I think about my parents, and my friends. I just hope what I am doing is right. I don't want anyone getting hurt because of me. We make it to the fire escape, and down to the ground level. I notice that Jill is thinking about something. She hasn't said a word, and all I can do now is hope that she knows what she's doing.

[END CHAPTER FOUR – MISSION]

We made it to the car, I was expecting something all black, streamlined, something out of a spy movie, but to see her driving an AE86 panda was something out of my street racing days.

"WHOA!! You race a little?" I ask.

She looks at me slightly confused and says, "Huh, what, this? No, no, no. I umm, acquired this from someone that was extremely charitable in my time of need."

I look at her, and say "charitable, huh? Somehow I don't think this person had much of a choice."

She smiled, and said, "well next time when a woman is walking all by her lonesome down the street I'm sure he won't think to try and harass her."

I shrug my shoulders, and exhale, "Never mind, never mind, I'm sure the less I know about all this the better." I say nonchalantly.

She chuckles briefly, and says "Now you're getting it. Honestly though, it's kind of late not to know everything, you're in this for the long haul."

I give her a raised eyebrow look, and say sarcastically, "Geez, since when were we a couple?"

We both laugh, at the same time. At that moment the engine starts up, and we drive off.

The car is tuned to perfection, the ride is smooth, and I drift off. I have no idea how long I was out. Looking around I can tell that we are out of city limits. As I am figuring out where we are, Jill says, "So you're awake, get it in now, because rest is going to be a limited commodity from here on in."

I straighten up in my chair, "Where are we headed to?" I ask. "You'll know when we get there; just relax, because we are going to be real busy soon." Jill says.

Looking around I notice a familiar portion of the landscape in the distance. I sit straight up, "WAIT! We're going to my uncle's house?"

Jill just smiles, and says, "Well, it looks like someone is ready for some work. Listen, we're not going to just go in; we're going to have ourselves a little stake out. Do you have anything to eat or drink in that bag of yours?"

I look down at the backpack, and start to open it up when I realize I didn't pack anything like that. "No, just the essentials, but there is a convenience store about a mile up on the right, but it will take us off the direct path. It's a full service station, so we can pretty much get what we need there. Before you say anything I have cash, I withdrew everything I had based on the thought that I may be getting into things that would make it not a good idea to use something electronic."

As Jill makes the turn to the convenience store, she says "I guess your uncle was right about you. You really are a smart guy. I know you're worried about him, I am too. We are going to find out what happened, okay."

We pull up to the store, and as we get out of the car I say, "Jill, thanks. I just want you to know I am with you all the way."

Jill walks off, but looks back quickly and smiles. I know what's in store isn't going to be easy, but I'm not someone that will quit, or be beaten so easily. I will find you Uncle!

After gathering the supplies needed, we load up the vehicle, and drive off back towards the house. Jill seems tense; I guess she's worried about what's going to happen. "Look when we get to our stake out a spot I am going to need you to keep a cool head, and not do anything but, observe the surroundings. We will have our moment to get in there; we just have to be patient. Do you understand?" I simply shrug my shoulders and say, "Okay, I am just going to watch. I will follow your lead."

We pull over after driving for about 20 minutes. Jill hands me a pair of binoculars that we got from the store. I can see my Uncle's house from here. We must be about a quarter mile from the residence.

"Jill, I know that I said that I was going to follow your lead, but we have been here for the last two hours, and no one has shown up here."

As I said that, a light turned on in the house, and the door opened. Could my Uncle be there now?

"Hey, we need to go there now, he is back", I shouted.

Jill then said, "James, you're an idiot! Pay attention!"

Now, how could this be? That's not my Uncle coming out of the house!

Jill speaks again, "They are searching high and low for him you know. I have been staking this place out for the last couple weeks. I know they are looking for something, but it seems they haven't found whatever it is that they are looking for."

Just at that moment a car pulls up, and a mysterious person gets into the passenger seat, and takes off. Jill begins to move, "Get in the car, we're moving in now, you're driving. I need you to drive past the house and slow down so I can get out. I need you to park a little further up, and wait for my signal to come in. Do you understand what I am asking you to do?"

I say, "Yes I got it. I will wait for your signal."

We drive towards the house; I turn down the road, and slow down just enough for Jill to take off running out of the car. I proceed to drive up a few more houses and park. It's been about five minutes, and then I see the porch light flick on and off a few times. I guess I should have asked what the original signal was supposed to be, but at this point I don't care. I grab my bag, and run down to the house. My heart is racing; I feel like I can barely contain myself. I know by coming here I will find something that will let me know what has happened to him.

I get to the front door, and it's open. I've been here so many times as a kid, but now it feels like I am walking in for the first time. Everything feels so different. So many memories, but none feel like they tie to this house, or its past.

Then I hear Jill, "James get in here now, and close the damn door!"

I walk in, and close the door behind me. I can't believe I'm back here. The stairs to the right that lead up to the old guest room where I would stay as a kid. The smell of the banister wood is truly nostalgic. As some of the feelings come rushing back in, it is interrupted almost immediately by Jill. "James, let's get these laptops charged up. Do you know if your Uncle kept any computer equipment, blank CD's, thumb drives, anything we can use to back up anything important?"

I thought for a second, and said, "Yea, if there is anything like that it would be upstairs in his room. I'll go, and I promise I won't linger."

Jill says, "Okay, but hurry, we need to get in and out of here."

I hurried up the stairs; I took a brief second to check out my room. It was trashed. Whoever was here was definitely looking for something, but if my Uncle was working for these people, then wouldn't all of his research be in the most obvious of places like in his office, and for that matter why does Jill have the most obvious of items like their work laptops. Perhaps I need to be a little more careful of Jill. I will have to keep my senses sharp around her. I walk into my Uncle's room. The immediate area is in tatters. Bed flipped, shelves knocked over, I guess the movies aren't based too far off from reality in this regard.

Jill yells, "Hey, I thought you said you weren't going to linger, did you find anything useful?"

"Not yet, this place is destroyed!" I shout.

Just then I find an internal laptop hard drive. It's an internal SATA, so I am guessing that they missed this during their search, or found nothing of interest on here, either way it's a start.

Upon further investigation of the mess, I found a USB drive, and an external USB HDD reader.

"I found a USB Drive. I am coming down" I yelled.

On my way down I see the picture of my Dad, and Uncle as kids hanging up on the wall right beside the one with my Uncle and I. I quickly remove both from the frames, and head downstairs. I can hear Jill in the kitchen area. I see she has the laptops plugged in, and booted up.

I pull out the USB drive, and say "Jill, catch."

Without as much as a glance she catches the USB drive without almost looking at it. Just who is she, where is she from, and why was she working for my Uncle as an assistant, she seems more like a bodyguard than a scientist.

It seems that Jill has already locked onto something, "Okay, I've found something of interest. It seems that your Uncle was working on theories revolving around the Hadron Collider. Not only that, but he has been going there seemingly once a quarter. All the dates are here, but nothing more than that. Some of his documentation is here, but again, nothing, wait no wait there is something. Embedded video within the documentation, I thought the file size was huge for word files."

We watched the videos for the next couple of hours. The videos are mind blowing; theories that are in my Uncle's journal, in some form or another are shown to actually work. Upon one of the videos I see something that startles me a bit.

I say, "Wait, go back a few seconds, and pause it when you see the guys in the suits."

Jill pans back about 10 seconds and freezes the frame.

"Right there, those two! They came to talk to me after graduation, and offered me an internship based on my Uncle's recommendation. The man to the right is Steve."

Jill stands up, and looks at me with a look of concern. She says, "That is Steve Bentclay. He's the president of Parasol Inc.'s Therapeutic cloning department. He is a senior member of the board, also oversees other research and development departments within Parasol Inc., and other companies heavily invested in by Parasol. I don't know how to tell you this, but your Uncle, and Bentclay did not see eye to eye on most things, but the other board members saw a future in your Uncle's research. I want to say more, but for now we get this backed up, pack up, and get out of here before anyone else shows up."

We gather up the laptops, and start packing up. As we're about to open the door to leave we hear someone walking up to the landing of the doorway, and a voice says, "Mr. Jonathan, are you home finally? It's your landlord Mr. Martin; your brother was here looking for you a few months ago, but we have not seen you for some time. Hello? Is someone there?"

Jill looks over at me putting her finger to her lips signaling me to be quiet. A few moments later we hear the landlord walk away from the house. Jill whispers, "Okay, let's go."

As we walk to the car Jill seems pre-occupied. "Jill is everything okay?" I ask.

She doesn't say anything; she just seems to be in thought. We get inside the car, and start to drive off. Jill looks upset; she turns and looks at me for a second.

"Jill what's the matter?" I ask.

Jill says, "I can't believe he said that he was giving you a job based on your Uncle's recommendation. It was all a lie! There would have never been anyway, ANYWAY THAT YOUR UNCLE WOULD HAVE DONE THAT!!!"

Jill is obviously upset about my meeting with Steve.

"James, you have to understand that this was all set up to watch you, to find a clue to where your Uncle is. They've been watching you, and possibly your family as well. Our primary focus is to find your Uncle, and nothing else!"

[END CHAPTER FIVE – RECONNAISSANCE]

I am in a state of disbelief. What kind of situation am I in right now? "Jill, I need to know what is really going on, right now!"

Jill says, "I will tell you everything, but right now we have to make sure that we are not being followed. I am going to need you watch for anything suspicious. If any vehicle follows for more than a mile let me know, understand?!"

I sit back in the chair, and say "Yes, I got it."

A minute and a half goes by, and I say, "Jill we have someone that hasn't changed lanes behind us, and they have been pretty steady in their distance between us.

Jill looks back, then looks forward, and says, "Hold on we are going to test something, if the car slows down, with us, then we are going to speed up, got it?"

Jill slows down, and a slew of honks begins, the tailing car drives past us.

Jill says, "Okay, did you see what kind of car it is?

I respond with, "Yes, I got it. It's a Chevy Equinox, Silver."

Jill looks at me and says, "Okay, I need you to watch it, do not take your eyes of it, we're going to speed up now!"

I exclaim, "Got it!"

Jill begins to speed up, she passes the tailing Equinox and gets off onto the highway ramp. We're doing at least 80 mph.

Jill shouts, "Do you see anything?"

I am scanning the area like crazy, "No I don't see anything matching that vehicle. Where are we going to now?" I ask.

"Right now we have to stay on the road until we're sure that we weren't being followed. After we confirm that we are not being tailed we will pull off to a motel, so we can plan our next move, and get some rest."

It's been about 5 minutes, and now I am noticing that the Equinox is behind us.

I say, "Jill I don't know how, but I think that the Equinox is behind us now."

"Hang tight, let's not do anything too hasty, I'm sure that there is more than one of those out there on the road right now. Let's let it catch up with us, and get a description of the driver, and any other passengers." Jill says.

Jill pulls in the far right lane, and the Equinox pulls ahead on the left. A single driver passes us by with two kids in the back, and with that a big sigh of relief from us both. A few miles up we found an exit that leads to a motel. We walk into the motel, and at the front desk, we see an attendant. She's an older woman at least in her sixties.

I say to her, "Good evening, ma'am would you happen to have a room available for the night?" She looks up at us with the biggest brightest smile, and says, "Oh my, yes. Hehehe, you two are such an attractive couple, are you models?"

I got tongue tied a bit, and then Jill says, "What us? Please, my little brother here, he wishes he was good looking."

Then front attendant smiles even bigger, "Oh, I see, so that's what I'm sensing here. I could tell that you were close, I'm sorry for the confusion." She said.

Then I said, "Yeah I could never be with a hag like her, but you wouldn't happen to be available would you ma'am?"

The front attendant said, "OHOHOHOHOHOHO, my word, you wouldn't know what to do with a woman like me, or would you?" She puts her hand on my hand, and Jill laughingly says,

"Oh, maybe I should leave you two alone for a while, and I'll just bring our things in hehehehe."

I pull my hand back quickly and say, "No,no,no Sis, I will grab all the bags, let's go dear sister."

The front attendant says, "You two have a great night." Then she looks at me with a wink in her eye, "And if you change your mind I'll be down here waiting for you."

Jill says, "Ooh-la-la, going to turn my little brother into a man?"

Then I start to push Jill out the door, and say, "Come dear sister let's not doddle."

We make it up to the 3rd floor, and unpack the bags with the laptops.

Jill says, "Okay, we've got at least twelve hours before we have to make our next move, the only question is what, and to where. We have to be exactly sure that the next move we make is going to help us track down the location of your uncle, or finding another location that will, one, provide us with a strong set of clues to our next location, and allow us to collect our thoughts. No offense but I don't know how well you can hold yourself in something more than a fist fight. By the way where did you learn to fight?"

I look down for a second, and say, "Well you probably wouldn't believe me, but my Uncle actually showed me how to throw my first punch. My Dad wasn't too happy about it at the time, but it all happened at the end of my second grade year during summer vacation. I was down the street playing with a girl that lived a couple houses down from where my uncle lived, and yea I guess you can say I liked her a lot; well anyway there were these other kids that came up started to pick on us, I don't know what we were doing, but all I remember is that they got off their bikes and started to pick on her. I tried to jump in and stop them, but I got my clock cleaned. When I got back to my uncle's house he saw me pretty messed up. He asked what happened, so I told him, and from there on for the next couple of summers my uncle taught me a mix of kickboxing, and Wu-Shu Kung Fu at my family's house. I thought it was a little strange that I never got to go back to my uncle's place, but after a while I didn't pay it any mind. The training ended when my Father found out that I was learning how to fight Now thinking on it I guess I can understand. I'm sure my Father would have wanted to be the one to show me how to throw a punch or two. From that point on, I didn't see my uncle as much. I mean the communication wasn't cut, but it was definitely limited. From there I trained at local schools for the next 10 years in jujitsu and different variations of karate. Well that's that."

Jill smiles, "Yes, your uncle knows how to throw a punch. He always seemed, you know, like the non-fighting type. He was just a quiet person with his hands in his pockets all the time. I guess you can never judge a book by its cover."

Jill pulls out the journal from her bag, and sits down on the bed opening it up to the first page. Jill says, "You know going over this first page here, reminds me of the first time I saw him writing in it. This whole journal has been based off a dream he had. He was a man consumed with his theories he was developing. It consumed him so much that he was putting off contract obligations within the research and development section with Parasol INC. The computations, advanced mathematical algorithms were out of this world, and I was able to witness one, personally. It changed my world; he (she pauses for a moment) changed my world. What do you think you know about this world, the universe for that matter? I can tell you it is not what it seems. There is so much more. I want you to know that your Uncle means a lot to me, he is my friend. He was one of the few people that I would confide in."

Jill stands up and begins to pace around the room, "He had a small circle of friends. I haven't been able to contact any of them for the last couple of weeks. When your uncle disappeared we all starting drifting apart, I quit the main branch of Parasol, but stayed on as a contractor. I want to know what happened to him, we need to find him."

I could see the look in her eyes, she was sincere. The way she spoke, I could not hear any waiver in her voice, she was being honest. For now, I have to trust her. We both have the same goal. After we find my Uncle, however, how will things change? It doesn't matter, but for now we have a common goal.

I sit down beside Jill, and I put my hand on her shoulder and say to her, "Jill I know this is hard for you, but I am going to need to know everything, and now. Let's start with Steve Bentclay. I need to fully understand the history of bad blood between them, and I guess anyone else that my Uncle may have crossed throughout the last couple of years."

Jill lets out a deep sigh, and says, "It was only Bentclay that had issues, mainly because your Uncle didn't have to deal with anyone else directly. Eventually all the projects that he and I worked on throughout the years were either completed on time, or way ahead of schedule. He stopped procrastinating, because your Uncle's main concern was the journal. Bentclay caught wind of your Uncle's side project and objected him using government funds for his own personal research. Your uncle said he would quit, he claimed that his research would benefit mankind, to help us with our species evolution, and also how it is all tied with the origin of the universe, the Big Bang. Basically the committee found out that your Uncle wanted to quit, and they begged him to stay. For the most part these higher-ups believed in your Uncles ability, and recognized that his genius was one in seven billion. It was a relationship they couldn't afford to lose to someone else. Your Uncle was granted funding for his side project dubbed "Infinite Possible".

We spend the rest of the night reviewing the documentation on the laptops. I feel like we're getting nowhere. It's around 2am and I am starting to drift off, and then my mind switches on, I remember the laptop external hard drive that I found with the internal reader.

"Jill!" I shout.

Jill is startled, "What?! You scared me half to death!"

I say, "I found another Hard Drive at my Uncles house, I wasn't sure if it was discarded because they had already deemed it not worth their time, or they missed it when they tore through the place. Before you get upset with me, I didn't say anything because at that moment I wasn't sure if I could totally trust you."

Jill takes the drive and the reader from me. She hooks it up to the laptop, and starts to scour through the files. In the midst of the clicking Jill turns to me and says, "I'm not mad at you, especially after everything that you've been through, but if we are going to make it through this we need to be totally honest with each other, and share any and all information. Got it?"

I walk over and sit beside her, "I got it Jill. We are a team."

Jill is running through the files like a mad woman. About twenty minutes into it Jill says "I found something, a file, but it's password protected. This might be a lead; any ideas?"

I sat up and thought; only one word came up, so I say "Courage". Jill says, "Courage?"

I say "Yea, he was always talking about being courageous in your actions, that it takes courage to bring change to oneself, and the world."

Jill says, "I wish I knew your Uncle like you did, let's try that!"

The key strokes are put in, C-O-U-R-A-G-E. The file opens. First the word file opens up, and then the screen goes black. Jill and I look at each other, but then it seems the laptop has booted back up again, and now the most incredible thing happens. I see my Uncle. Jill and I are both awestruck, and both of us are frozen. My Uncle looked tired, but then he starts to speak, it's a prerecorded video.

"The date is November 14th 2014. I am about to embark on what will be the most ground breaking, no life changing scientific discovery known to man. It will forever change the course of human history, and that of the universe itself. If this video has fallen into the hands of my nephew, or my assistant Jill, this video will end and you will be lead to another screen with a password that only James will know. James do you remember the story I told you about the woman that got away, but for all intents and purposes, it was the best thing that could have happened, because I got to meet you? I got to watch you grow into a fine person. You're every bit as intelligent as I am, and I know that you know what I am talking about. I miss you so much buddy. I have no idea how long it will be until we see each other, or rather if we even see each other again.

Jill if you're watching this, find my nephew, keep him safe. I know there is more to you than meets the eye, and that's why I know you can protect him if something should happen to him. Teach him everything that you've learned from me, and in turn he will amaze you, that I can guarantee. Finally, James if you're with Jill and you both are watching this, then I want to apologize to both of you for whatever ordeals that you've had to face. I know that this task of finding me has probably been a challenge, but I assure you that I will be, I am fine. James, I hope you told your parents how much you love them, and I hope your dad still isn't mad at me for, you know, being me. I miss my little brother so much.

James I am counting on you, and Jill I am relying on you. Please Jill, keep him away from Steve Bentclay. He is not to be trusted. You know about his past; the people he has working under him. How he has been able to move the way he has is still unknown. You know that is why I had to leave. James listen to me, nothing good will come from that man. No matter what happens, you must not accept anything from him. Well, I have to go. If you two are watching this, and you come to where I tell you, you will find me eventually. Beware the shadows, listen to your reflection, and have courage to see everything to the end. Goodbye......"

The video kicked off some white noise for a moment, then the screen went black. A flashing cursor pops up on the black screen beside the words that read *ENTER PASSWORD*.

As I stare at the blinking cursor for the next few seconds I can feel Jill looking at me ready to say something. "Well James, what is it? What's the password?

I looked down for a minute, and said "I don't know. It's been so long since he told me any stories, and most of the time I just wanted to learn to fight, and blow stuff up in the back yard. What can I say; I was just a boy at the time. I had no idea anything like this would happen."

Jill sounds frustrated says, "Well, not to be rude, but we don't have much time, I need you to think. Come on, we need to…."

I screamed "SHUT UP! God, oh my God, I am so sorry. I am trying really hard here."

Jill takes a deep breath and says, "It's okay, let's be calm here. Let's take a break, and get some food. There's a 24hr Pancake Palace in the parking lot. What do you say; take me out for some food."

I look at her crazy, "Like a date, what is up with you?" Jill looks at me with a smile and says, "Well I have a thing for siblings, C'mon."

I say, "ewwwwww". Jill grabs me by the arm, and we walk to the Pancake Palace. As we walk across the motel parking lot Jill says nothing, but just has a smile on her face.

I guess it was nice to hear from my Uncle, and then she says, "I haven't seen your Uncle in about a year. At first I thought he was just off on something top secret, but then I just got worried when he didn't at least call after 4 months. That's usually the time he resurfaces from anything, you know, that he can't talk about. We're going to find him soon, I just know it."

I can't help but to smile. For the first time in a while I feel hope again. "Jill, I am glad I met you, but there is one thing that bothers me."

"What's that?" Jill asked.

I looked at her squarely, "Back in the alley when we first fought, I thought for sure I had you beat, why did I get knocked out?"

Jill just smiles and says, "A girl never reveals her secrets, but I will tell you something about the alley that is important. When I kissed you, I have to admit you think fast on your feet, and you're a good kisser. You must have someone special in your life, huh?"

I find my face heating up a bit "Wow, thanks. Hehehe, and no, there is no one special in my life right now."

Jill says, "Good, for the next hour or so let's enjoy our date then."

It didn't hit me at first, but this was probably the only time in a long time that she has been able to be, well normal. We took the booth that faced the skyline. As we ate, and conversed, we watched the sunrise together. For a minute it felt like I was normal again, like a weight had been shed from my body. I could think clearly for the first time since this whole ordeal began.

I pay the waitress, and leave a tip. Jill and I get up to leave, and now I remember the story of what my Uncle was talking to me about. Jill walks away and notices that I haven't moved. I can't believe that I didn't remember.

"James, is everything okay?" She asks.

I look up at her with a grin, "Couldn't be better, because I remember what my Uncle was talking about. I know the password."

Jill's face lit up. She grabs my hand, and we bolt out the door. We are running at top speed up to the room.

Jill says, "Hurry, enter the password!" I sit down praying that this is right. I only have one chance at this I type, "L-o-r-r-a-i-n-e" The screen kicks off an alert in the background "ALL DRIVES WILL BE WIPED IN 30 SECONDS, PLEASE RE-ENTER PASSWORD"

Jill says, "Did you type it in wrong, come on we can't lose this!" I think, and now it all comes back to me.

FLASHBACK:

Jonathan: No problem, we just blew up a couple items in the back yard. The kid has a talent for demolition, hahaha! Don't worry, it's a controlled environment. Okay, I understand. Talk to you later Lori.

COUNT DOWN 5 – 4 – 3 – 2… I type L-o-r-i

PASSWORD CONFIRMED!!!!

The screen goes black again. Another huge sigh of relief fills the air, then a punch.

"OWWW DAMN IT!!!" I say.

Jill chuckles, "Don't do that again"

I rub my arm, "Okay, okay, seesh, hehe."

At that moment, a green cursor pops up on the screen, and a computerized voice says, "Please plug your GPS unit into the console, and prepare for download."

I look at Jill and say "Do you have a GPS on you? She goes for her bag and pulls a variety of items; a satellite phone, tablet, Gameboy with Super Mario World, and a GPS.

Jill says, "Here, take this." I take the GPS, and say "Thanks, but after this, I am playing that when I'm done." pointing at the Gameboy.

Jill looks at me shaking her head. She sighs, and says "Okay, when we're done. You better not beat my high score; I'll be so mad at you!"

I hook up the GPS to the laptop, and instantaneously it started to upload the information to the GPS. Then the Computer generated voice says, "UPLOAD COMPLETE, ALL FILES ARE TO BE WIPED IN 3 … 2

… 1…" I pull the GPS off the cable. "PURGE IN PROCESS, PURGE COMPLETE!!" I turn on the menu to the GPS and look for favorites.

"I got it!" I exclaimed.

Jill starts to move, packing as fast as she can. "Let's go!" She says.

I know this is what she has been waiting for, and so have I. As I watch Jill move at mach speed, I can hear my mind racing at a million thoughts a second. I am excited, and at the same time, a feeling of uncertainty is setting in. I hope that this is nothing and that soon I will get to see my uncle again.

[END CHAPTER SIX – REVELATION]

We have the lead that we've been looking for in a big way! Jill is running downstairs, as I am going through and packing up the last of our items. I see the journal on the bed. I place the last few items in the bag, and I grab the journal and sit down.

I let out a big sigh, "PHEW, uncle, I'm coming to see you. I hope you're okay."

I open the journal to the back to re-read the passage that was written down. The last day and a half has been full of riddles and clues, so I figure that this must be important, otherwise it wouldn't be in here.

> *"A place in time that finds a moment of eternity shall see the futures past momentarily. What is viewed is nothing more than a dream of events for tomorrow."*

I have no idea where he is going with this, or who would talk like this. It's an odd thought that feels like it makes sense, even though I can't make heads or tails of it. I grab the complimentary note pad and pen from the motel, and I write it down.

At that moment Jill yells out, "James! Let's go! Hurry up and check out already!"

I yell back "I'm coming, I'm coming!"

I throw my backpack on and do a quick idiot check around the room. Good, we didn't forget anything. I clutch onto my Uncle's journal tightly. I have a feeling I am not going to get it back once Jill sees me with it. I walk out of the room and with the door closed behind me the reality hits me even harder now that I am going to find out everything. I head down to checkout, and the front desk receptionist is at the breakfast bar helping out an older gentleman carry his food to his table.

He hurries back to the desk, "Sorry about that man." He says.

As he pulls up his screen to check out he says, "Name please."

I say, "James"

He looks at me funny for a moment, and I ask "Is everything okay?"

The receptionist says, "Well, nothing wrong per say, but it seemed weird that the night attendant only logged you in with a first name, I mean I saw your key number from your card."

I ask, "Why is that weird. I mean your attendant was a little old lady, who I may add, umm had a lot of energy."

He smiled and said, "Hahahahaha yeah that's Ethel for ya. Sir, just to let you know, and it's because I'm a vibe person, and I can tell you and your friend out there aren't bad people, so it's with a heavy heart that I warn you, and you didn't hear this from me, but there were two women, and man in suits looking for your two this morning. They didn't present ID's, but I didn't like their vibe at all. I told them that I don't know anyone here by that name. They didn't leave a card, they just walked out. Scary, right?"

Fear sets all over my body, I had to keep calm. I said, "Thank you; here's the money, and keep the change."

As I handed the receptionist the money he said, "Thanks, and Good luck bro."

I hurried as fast as I could out the front door. Without saying a word to Jill I threw my bags in the back.

Jill gets in the driver side seat, and says, "What's wrong did you see a ghost or something? Oh, I get it; the nice old lady wasn't done with you yet?! Hahahahaha!"

I say "DRIVE!"

Jill turns with a concerned look on her face and says "What's wrong I was just playing?"

I say, "Look you have to drive now! The front desk guy said that there were two women and a man looking for us. They left no ID, or cards, and they asked for me by name. DRIVE!"

Jill puts the keys in and revs the engine, pops the car into reverse, and we speed off. As Jill is driving I pull out the GPS, and turn it on.

SET DESTINATION > FAVORITES

It's a longitude, and latitude set of coordinates. The GPS says, "**DRIVE FOR 100 miles west on interstate 80**".

A hundred miles west; now we have a destination. I have no idea what we are going to face along the way; all I know is that there is no stopping us! I turn and look at Jill and say, "Are you ready? I'll keep a look out for anyone following us." Jill kept her gaze forward;

"James, listen I don't know how things are going to turn out here from now on, but I want you to know that, (sigh), I want you to know that I care about you, and I promise you that I will never betray you. After all, this is over, and we get your uncle, let's go on a real date, my treat."

In the midst of the stress induced situation, I find a way to smile, and I say "I can't wait. Let's go somewhere where we can get a funnel cake. Something tells me that you're good at a BB gun duck shoot and I want a giant foam finger."

This is probably the last laugh we are going to have together in a while. Jill and I chuckle for a moment, but it is so weighed down by the reality that we are not alone anymore.

We've been driving for an hour now, and there is no sign of anyone tailing us. I sit back in the seat, and say, "Jill do you mind if we pull off for a second? I need a Seven Hour Energy. I haven't had one since college."

Jill shakes her head, "No, we're making good time, and so far there is no immediate danger. It would be a bad idea to deviate from our current course."

A grin comes over my face because I notice something that she doesn't, and I say, "We're about to hit empty on the tank, we need gas."

Jill looks down, "DAMN IT! Okay, we fill up, and get the hell on; no lingering understood!?"

I nod, "Yes, I got it; in and out no problem." I say.

We see a gas station sign, and take the next exit. We pull up to the gas station, and identify the number on the pump. "Alright I'll go in and put fifty in number five, Jill, are you going to be okay?"

Jill says "yeah, yeah, hurry up we got to go!"

I walk into the convenience store and it's pretty empty. I see the front clerk behind the register. I pull out fifty dollars, and tell him, "Number 5 please." I walk back outside giving Jill the signal to pump. I go back into the store. As I am grabbing some waters, and some snacks, and head to the register I hear a helicopter in the background. My gut tells me it's time to run.

I hand the cashier a ten, and say, "Keep the change!" I run out of the store towards the car, I see Jill already inside starting up the car. "James, get in here, hurry!" She must be thinking the same thing that I'm thinking right now.

We peel out onto the road. "James, I need you to keep an eye on the sky. We need to make sure that the helicopter is not following us.

I say, "Jill pull over, if we want to be sure that we're not being followed right now then this will be the best way to do it. Jill nods, and pulls over onto the shoulder. The helicopter flies overhead, and continues its course.

Jill says, "Sorry I got ahead of myself, and got a little paranoid. Let's give it a few minutes, then make our way to the destination on the GPS."

There is no sound of the helicopter in the distance anymore, Jill pulls out and we start driving again. Being in the flow of normal traffic has somewhat calmed this tense situation.

Suddenly the GPS says, "**Good bye**", the screen blinks out, and reboots.

"James what did you do?" Jill says in an irritated manner.

I am looking at the GPS and the screen is starting to come back on, and I say "I didn't do anything, your GPS got all weird on me, and started over on its own." The GPS showed the welcome screen, but the voice changed from the default that was used, and it said, "**In twenty miles take exit 146b**."

Jill and I both look at each other slightly confused, then Jill says, "Okay I am not going to argue with anything your uncle gave us. Let's trust in him right now, okay?"

At this moment Jill's words allow for my mind to clear, and I say, "You're right, let's go."

You can feel it in the air, it's a sense of the beginning of the end. Jill and I have been silent the whole time in the car. We are both so focused on the GPS, waiting for the next set of instructions to be spoken that I have not been paying attention to the road to see if anyone is following us. I look out from the rear view mirror to see if anything is out of the ordinary. I cannot identify anything following us, and nothing seems to be out of the norm.

As I take my eyes off the road I look down at the GPS, and say, "Jill, we've got three more miles until exit 146b. I haven't seen anything that looks like anyone is tailing us."

Jill says, "Good we're almost there. I need you to be ready for anything."

I nod, and say, "I'm ready."

"**IN ONE MILE TAKE EXIT 146b**", the GPS says. Jill accelerates, and pulls into the far right lane onto the exit ramp. "**IN FIVE HUNDRED FEET TURN RIGHT ONTO POPPLER STREET, YOUR DESTINATION IS ON THE RIGHT**" The GPS says. Jill turns right into a seemingly abandoned lot, it's mostly dirt and trees. In the distance you can see a gated fence area with a building further in at the back of the lot. Suddenly the GPS shuts off on its own once again. This time Jill and I wait for it to reboot. The GPS screen flashes again, as if it's going to turn on all the way, but then the screen goes black, and a set of numbers are displayed "45-87-101-1-19".

I say the numbers out loud as they are coming across the screen, and Jill right along with me. The screen fades, and reads, "............. SYSTEM WIPE IN.... 2.......1 ...... SYSTEM WIPE IN PROGRESS....... GOOD LUCK".

Jill and I immediately get out of the car. Jill says, "It looks like your uncle took no chances of leaving a trail to be followed. Let's get this car out of sight. We'll move it into the trees over here, it will provide good camouflage. Let's take the bags with us." After moving the car a few hundred feet away from the gate entrance, we grab our bags out of the car, and walk to the gate. Upon inspection of the gate we see the gate is magnetically locked.

"Jill, do you see a keypad, or anyway through here?" I ask.

Jill hands me her bags, and pulls out a bottle of water. She pours a little into her hands, and says, "I need you to back up a couple of feet."

I stand back about ten feet from where I was, and she tosses the water on the side of the fence. Immediately you can see the electrical current, and hear the crackle of electricity. Jill says, "Well, climbing isn't an option."

Just then a voice from a distant PA system says, "You two are trespassing on private property. If you aren't Girl Scouts selling cookies, then get the hell out!

You've got five seconds to comply! 5 …. 4…… 3……
2……, then I scream "WAIT, I AM LOOKING FOR MY
UNCLE. DOCTOR EDWARDS, DOCTOR JONATHAN
EDWARDS!!"

At that moment an electronic buzz started, and I bolt for
the entrance. As I go to open the door, Jill yells out,
"WAIT YOU IDIOT!" The words fall on deaf ears as the
door swings open, I rush on through. Jill sprints, and
tackles me to the ground; just then the gate door
automatically closes on its own.

Jill says, "You idiot! We don't know who is in here, and
also we don't know if there any traps on the premises.
Get your act together, NOW!!" The voice over the PA
system said, "You don't have anything to worry about,
come to the building directly in front of you. Hurry, we
don't have all night."

Jill and I hustle to the building entrance. There is a
camera with a PA speaker. I step up and say, "Hello,
umm we're here."

There is nothing, no voice. Jill and I stand there for
about a minute staring at the door, and then, *CLICK*.
The sound of a single bolt action reloading right behind
us, and then a voice says, "You've piqued my interest,
which is why I am only going to ask you, once; how do
you know Doctor Edwards, and lastly how did you find
this place?"

"Jill." I say. "I am going to need you not to say anything, trust everything that I am about to do. We don't need any brain matter over the walls here."

The man's voice chuckles, "Hehehehe smart kid; so what are you going to do now? My patience is running thin."

I laugh for a second and say, "It's amazing, but I remember hearing your voice. I know you've been to my uncle's house before; it's been such a long time Big Brother Anthony."

Then the man replies, "Well, I'll be damned. I've only had one little brat call me that, and that was over ten years ago. James, you've grown up." He sighs, and says, "Turn around, both of you."

He is no longer pointing the gun at us which is great. He has a weird smirk across his face, and then he says, "What are you doing here? Man, the last time I saw you, you were just learning how to fight after getting beat up by those kids up the street."

Anthony pulls his rifle behind his back, and extends his hand to shake. The moment we shake hands, I can see that something is wrong, it's written all over his face.

He turns his gaze toward Jill, and asks, "Who might you be?" Jill quickly responds with her name, "Jill". He asks, "Jill, huh? So you're the assistant he was going off about for the last couple of years. Well, he was right about one thing."

Jill says, "Right about what?" As Anthony looked her up and down once he says, "Nothing, it's nothing. Come on inside you two, oh wait, you need the pass code to get in."

Anthony pulls out a handgun, and says, "Look, if you truly are who you say you are then this part should not be a problem, and too much has been going on lately for me to trust someone that I haven't seen in over ten years, and you're with a person I have never met. So now we are back to this. If you were given instructions on how to get here, then the combination would have been part of it, so James if you don't mind, could you open the door, please?"

I can hear the hammer of the gun cock back; I know that if I do not recall the numbers correctly we are all dead. I approach the keypad on the side of the door, and enter 45-87-101-1-19, and the red light that is flashing dims and then turns green. The electronic popping sound of the locking mechanism was the indication that the door was now accessible.

Just then, Anthony pushes through us all with a boisterous laugh and says, "Hahahahaha, just had to make sure, come in, come in!"

Jill looks highly pissed off says to me, "You know this guy? I'm going to kill him!"

She walks inside. I really hope she's not going to try anything. This is where we are supposed to be, so I guess Anthony is the key to our next clue. As we walked into the building, we can see that it is a research facility. To the immediate right, there are rows of tables with computers as far as the eye can see. Some of the screens are on; it looks like they are running mathematical equations.

Anthony says. "Hey, do you have your Uncle's journal?"

At that moment Jill says, "Wait how would you know about it?"

Anthony stops and walks back towards our direction; he stops, looks at us, and shakes his head. He had the demeanor of a parent mentally scoffing at a child who had just said something ridiculous.

Anthony says, "Do you really think just because you are his assistant that he had that journal of his when you started working for him? Give me a break; stop being so suspicious. Please tell me that you didn't think that you were the only one involved in his work as a scientist? You do know that he has been a scientist for as long as you two have been alive, right?"

Jill's fist relaxed, she shifted her body to the wall, and leaned back.

Jill exhaled, she was just letting go of all the built up tension. The amount of time that it took to do the things she had to do to get to this point seems to have reached its apex, and then fallen off her back mentally.

She raises her head, turns to Anthony, and says, "Well, Jonathan's instructions brought us here, and I have placed my trust in everything that he has said, but with that said I don't know you, so how about you introduce yourself first, and then I will think about handing over the journal to you."

Anthony shakes his head, again posturing as an adult that must pander to the whims of a child. He says, "Well, well, it seems the good doctor has chosen a worthy assistant to uphold the cause."

Jill looks surprised and says, "What cause?"

Anthony chuckles and says, "Hehehe, if you don't get it by now, then maybe I will just TAKE the journal, and send you two off, because without the journal you two can live normal lives, but I don't think that's an option you would willfully accept now would you?"

I turn to Jill, and say, "You know what it is. It's the reason Bentclay has his goons looking for us. Uncle J was going to change the world with his discoveries."

Anthony jumps up, and says, "Wait, Bentclay is looking for you? I am going to need to know everything that has happened up to this point."

For the next couple of minutes Jill explains everything, from the time that she became worried, and began to search for my Uncle, locating the journal to my location, Bentclay's approaching of me at the graduation, the agents, and the journey to this location.

Anthony takes a chair and sits down, and says, "James, so when Bentclay approached you was he with anyone?"

I thought back for a minute, and nodded my head, "Yes, I remember that there was a shorter woman, blonde hair, wavy, and there was also a guy about the same height as Bentclay, he was wearing shades, and whenever he wanted to talk to Bentclay he was always whispering in his ear."

Anthony stands up, "Damn, those are his direct advisors, or henchmen, however you want to look at this. They have a beat on you. They know what you look like now, and I am assuming they have been tailing you."

Jill stood up and says, "Yes, there was a moment where we thought we were being tailed, but it turned out to be nothing. However, at the motel we were staying at, the front attendant told James that there was someone that asked for him. The front attendant didn't give him any information, but he did give us a description that it was 2 women, and a man looking for us. I can only imagine that the two women were the ones that tried to run down James in the alley the night I met him."

Anthony looks at me and says, "So, no other descriptions, just two women and a man?"

Realizing that I made a mistake I say, "I didn't think to do anything else, but to get out of there once the front attendant told me; I didn't want to lose everything that we had obtained."

Anthony shakes his head, and says, "So your ignorance and your selfish actions have cost you, and now me the benefit of overall secrecy."

At the moment I am puzzled, "What do you mean selfish action?"

Anthony walks over to me, and grabs me by my shirt collar, and yells, "You idiot! You've probably brought them right here! Was there anything overhead like a helicopter flying overhead?"

I stuttered, Y-Y-Yes! However, it just kept on flying by, we had even pulled off on the shoulder to watch it go off into the distance. There were no other sounds of a helicopter, or any vehicles tailing us on the way here. We're fine."

He pushes me against the wall, and says, "You little brat, you stupid little brat. You and your girlfriend here have been tailed the whole time. When you were at your uncle's house did you really think that the surveillance would have stopped at just the searching of his house? They have had the whole area cased inside, and out. Bentclay is a man with seemingly unlimited resources, and he uses them indiscriminately. You've been tailed this whole time. They didn't act on it, because they want to find your uncle. It's only a matter of time before they think he's here! Wait here!"

Anthony lets go of my shirt, and walks into the next room.

Jill looks upset, "Damn it! How could I have been so blind? I should have known this trip here was too good to be true. We've been tracked this whole time. The dirt road out in front is going to have our tire tracks in the ground. DAMN IT!"

I look over at Jill, and say, "I'm sorry Jill if I hadn't come with you then you wouldn't have been distracted, and this whole situation probably wouldn't have happened."

Jill turns and looks at me, touches my shoulder, and says, "James no, this isn't your fault, the fact that you're a variable in this equation does not mean you were, or are a distraction. Without you I wouldn't have made it this far, WE wouldn't have made it this far. All we would have had were the thoughts of where your uncle could be, and not understanding at all what has been going on."

Her words were soothing, and made me realize something.

It made me realize that we haven't asked Anthony the most important question of all, so I yell out, "Anthony is my uncle alive?"

There's a second where for just a moment a feeling of eternal silence fills the room, but is instantly ended by

Anthony responding with the words, "YES! But he isn't here. Hurry and get over here, NOW!"

We walk into the next room, and see the camera monitors of the facility. Anthony says, "So far so good, but it's only a matter of time. I'm sorry about earlier, but the stress of knowing what's going to have to happen next got to me. You get ready, we are about to start Protocol Two."

Jill and I say at the same time, "Protocol Two?"

Anthony walks over to a computer in the far corner of the room, and enters a series of commands on the touch screen. A microphone and biometric hand scanner rise out of a console to the left of the computer.

Anthony says, "You two look to your right." At that moment the wall slides open to reveal an entrance that looked like an elevator door was behind it. "Alright, you two, I need you to get your stuff and head to the door, things are about to get interesting for all of us."

Jill looks at me and nods as if to tell me to go to the door. I don't think too much into it. Jill and I get our `bags and head to the door. At that very moment we hear Anthony say, "This is Blackmoon. Authorize sequence, Romeo, under, Nancy, Nancy, opera, Winston."

Then a computer generated voice, says, "**SEQUENCE ACKNOWLEDGED, PROJECT BURROWING PHOENIX ACTIVATED...... TOP SIDE FACILITY DESTRUCTION IN TWO MINUTES AREA DETONATION IMMINENT PLEASE EXIT TO INDICATED EVACUATION HIGH SPEED ELEVATORS.**

Anthony heads towards us by the elevator door. As we walk into the elevator, Anthony presses a sequence of numbers on the keypad inside the elevator, the two doors close, and then Anthony says, "Get ready to brace yourselves you two. You are about to enter into a world that you didn't even know existed."

Just then the elevator quickly descends. For about a minute the elevator continues to go further and further down, and then it stops. Then the computerized voice says, "**45 SECONDS UNTIL AREA DETONATION PLEASE EXIT TO INDICATED EVACUATION HIGH SPEED ELEVATORS.**" Anthony enters another series of entries on the keypad. A female computerized voice says, "**Voice recognition please. Please authorize.**"

Anthony says, "Charlie, Alpha, Peter, Charlie, Omega, Michael." Then the female computerized voice says, "**Voice recognition confirmed. Authorization INFINITE POSSIBLE activated.**" The door closes quickly, and chairs with seat belts rise up from the floor.

Anthony yells out, "Okay kiddies, time to strap in and hold tight."

Just then the computerized voice says, **"25 SECONDS UNTIL AREA DETONATION."**

We all strap ourselves in; the seats automatically turn 180 degrees, and WOOOOSH! We take off in a flash.

Jill is screaming, "What the hell?!"

Anthony is yelling out, "WOOOHOOOOO!", and I just try to keep from throwing up.

At that moment you can hear, **"5...... 4...... 3 ... 2.... 1 HAVE A GREAT DAY."** There was a slight vibration that surged through the elevator room we are all in, then a moment of acceleration.

Anthony, screams out, "Oh –Shiiiiiiiii, Computer this is Blackmoon! Close bomb blast doors sectors Bravo 2 Charlie, and Nemesis 3 Delta.

The Computer says, **"ACKNOWLEDGED! BOMB BLAST DOORS BRAVO 2 CHARLIE, and NEMESIS 3 DELTA CLOSING".**

The room became completely quiet. Just then the ride slowed down, and a computerized voice said, **"EVACUATION TO SECTION Z COMPLETE. PLEASE PREPARE TO STAND."**

An alarm goes off with a bright spinning orange light in the corner of the wall. The seats, prop us up, and the seatbelt's detach.

Jill and I look at each other, Anthony stands up, gets himself adjusted and says, "Welcome to your new home. I hope you like it because you are going to be here for a while. The good thing is that you won't be found down here. Heck, we're not even in the same state anymore."

Just as I am about to ask what's going on, the computerized voice says, "**WELCOME TO SECTION Z. DOOR LOCKS DISENGAGE IN TEN SECONDS. PLEASE WATCH YOUR STEP.**"

The door opens up, and we are in a small city underneath the ground.

Jill asks, "Is this a NORAD Facility?"

Anthony smiles, and says, "Yes, to a degree. This area was abandoned due to compliance issues, and Doctor Jonathan was able to negotiate this into his deal for his research. There are a few more that are joined together by a hyper-loop system like the one we just traveled in. If your Uncle is anywhere, it's going to be here."

I look at Jill, and say, "Now we are close, let's go."

Anthony says, "Follow me, I have a feeling that tonight we are going to have a family reunion."

We walk further into the facility, unsure of what future lies before us, but all I know is that this part of our journey is coming to an end."

[CHAPTER SEVEN END – INFINITE DISCOVERY]

Meanwhile, above ground, three shadowy silhouettes stand in the distance observing the fires of the facility.

A woman's voice speaks over a cell phone.

"Sir, the facility has been destroyed. It's only a matter of time before the local authorities, and media show up. What's our next course of action?"

(*Voice on the other end of the phone*), "Decem get out of there and report back to the extraction zone, we have another lead. Your hard work as always is appreciated, but if you continue to let them slip away, I will find someone else to replace you. Do not fail me again, do you understand agent?"

Decem says, "Yes, sir, failure is not an option, and the individuals will be caught." *CLICK*.

The phone hangs up, and Decem throws her fist into the air, screaming, "DAMN IT, DAMN IT, DAMN IT! Tres, Novem, we must capture the targets immediately!"

Agent Tres says, "What did Agent Primus say?"

Agent Decem lowers her eyes, and says, "Failure is not an option."

Tres approaches Decem, and says, "This is what you wanted, the role of squad captain, now it's yours, and you have to accept everything that comes with it. Novem, and I would not have recommended you for this role if you weren't capable, so get your head in the game! What's our next move?"

Decem pulls back, with a smirk on her face and says, "We head back to the extraction zone, it seems that we have a new lead to go on once we arrive."

Agents Novem, and Tres snap to attention, and say "Yes Ma'am!" All three agents get into the vehicle and drive off.

Agent Decem says, "Tres plug in the coordinates for the extraction zone into the GPS, they should have already sent the information over the secured line.

Tres responds with, "Got it. Coordinates set. Extraction point fifteen minutes from current position, I'm placing the GPS on the dashboard console screen.

Decem says, "Thanks Agent Tres." Tres says, "Stop thanking me for standard operating practices, this is what is supposed to happen."

Decem sighs, "Agent Tres, understood. However, Agent Tres if you try and correct a personality trait that is not placing you, or anyone on my team in danger, then I will handle the situation as insubordination, and I will put you on administrative leave. I will not tolerate someone trying to stifle my individualism while under my command! Do you get me?!"

Tres looks astounded, and says, "Yes ma'am."

"IN ONE MILE TURN RIGHT ONTO GIDDINGS LANE, AND KEEP RIGHT TO YOUR DESTINATION" The GPS says.

Agent Decem says, "Alright everyone, get ready! Novem I am going to need you to acquire the intel from our POC that should be at the extraction zone. Agent Tres, please ensure that we have the necessary gear ready to go in case of an air deployment. Once we arrive on site, we will have 5 minutes to gather up, and move out."

Agent Tres, and Novem say, "YES MA'AM!"

Decem has a smile on her face, she knows that this is her moment to take the lead and make herself a permanent leader.

Agent Decem thinks, "This is it! No time for mistakes. We are going to capture James, and the doctors' assistant by tonight. I will show that I am qualified; I will make Tres and Novem proud of me. They are my only family, and I will not fail them."

"IN FIVE HUNDRED FEET BEAR RIGHT, YOUR DESTINATION IS ON THE RIGHT" The GPS says.

Agent Decem pulls up to an abandoned looking building. The area is desolate with no signs of human traffic. The team steps out of the car, and waits. At that moment the door to the building opens up and a man walks out dressed in a suit, hat, and sunglasses. He is concealing his identity. There is a moment where all four individuals stare at each other.

Novem then steps in front of Decem, and says, "Are you the contact?"

The man in the suit says, "Agent Novem, Tres, and Decem it is a pleasure. I am your POC Agent. Please note that I am not using a code name; due to the nature of your current activity, I have been instructed to abstain from using my code name. This is by Agent Primus' instruction"

Agent Novem approaches the Agent, and is handed an envelope. Novem opens it up, and examines the contents of the information. A look of shock runs across his face.

The Agent then steps up to Novem, and says, "Good luck, you have 96 hours."

The Agent turns back and walks into the building. Novem walks back to Decem, and hands her the information. Decem's face too has a look of shock. In the information there is a set of longitude, and latitude coordinates.

Decem immediately runs to the car, and says, "Agent Tres where is the tablet?"

Agent Tres, says, "It's in the passenger console area, why, what information did you get?

Agent Tres, says, "Agent Decem the necessary items are packed and ready to go. Why are you in such a rush for the tablet?"

Decem hands the paper to Tres, and Tres says," Are you sure this is where they are at? How did they move there so fast? What's even out there"

Decem frantically logs into the tablet and says, "I need quiet!"

Tres locks up, and says, "Yes ma'am!"

Decem locks in the coordinates into the topography map application. She sits back and waits. The screen on the tablet changes, and the map is shown, Decem looks astounded.

Decem says, "Tres, Novem they crossed the state line two hundred miles east of here. Our priority is to know the logistics of the area. We now have a lock on them.

I don't know how they were able to travel such a distance in such a short amount of time, and without us noticing. We have to move right now. We will be moving by road. If we stay on the interstate, we will be able to arrive on site in 5 hours. All law enforcement will stay out of our way so speed is not an issue. Let's get to a facility where we can refuel and move."

Novem steps up towards Decem, and says, "Agent Decem I was told that we have 96 hours to complete this mission. Agent may I speak freely?"

Decem smiles, and says, "Of course."

Novem crosses his arms, and says, "Look, I feel that we are being setup here. Whether or not we complete the task here in the time frame allowed, I have a feeling that Primus is going to move before then, so we must keep our eyes open. This group here is the only group of people I will trust until all of this is over."

Agent Tres has a look of disbelief, and says, "Novem! How could you think that Primus would betray any of the Cardinal members? This attitude of yours is treasonous, and should be reported, but I am not in charge. Decem please handle this now."

Agent Decem just smiles, walks towards Novem, and turns to look at Tres. Decem then says, "How the hell could you say anything like that Tres?! All of us have been there for each other, and now you are questioning loyalties? Stop always going by the damn book, and go with your gut! When has Novem ever betrayed us? His analysis of all situations is always spot on, and his judgment is without question, so shut up now, or I will have you brought up on acts of misconduct."

Tres' face turns beet red, and Decem says, "Oh my, are you getting angry?" Decem turns and looks to Novem, and says, "Thank you Novem. Your concerns, thoughts, and insight are always welcome. No matter what please speak your mind. I will never look down upon you, or second guess your thought process."

Novem says, "Yes ma'am".

Decem says, "Tres, Novem lets go. We have 96 hours to complete our mission."

The team gets into the car, and drives away from the facility. Decem says, "Tres input the GPS coordinates, and make the call so we are not stopped by law enforcement. Once we refuel we will be on our way."

Decem pulls into a gas station, and Tres gets out to pump the fuel. Decem opens up the topography map on the tablet.

She turns to Novem, and says, "Novem is it me or does it seem like this destination is at a former military installation?"

Novem grabs the tablet, "Hmm, it seems that way. The facilities here were old training grounds for covert echelon groups like ours, mainly groups that were operating as the fourth echelon. Even these have been closed for years. There are rumors that there are a handful of NORAD facilities scattered throughout the area, however, these are just rumors."

Decem pulls back the tablet, and scans the screen, and says, "Hmmm, well there is no way to know for sure until we get there. If there is anything like that out there we won't have the equipment to scan the area with properly. With the situation the way it is we are probably cut from accessing that kind of information. Well, for now we'll take what we can get, and move from there."

Tres enters the car, and says, "The car has been refueled, what's our move?"

Decem says, "We get to the site, and survey the area. At this moment this is all we have to go on. From here on we trust in each other, and we will listen to each other. It's more than just following directive, follow your intuition, and if you see something stop and contact the rest of the team. Do you understand?"

Tres, and Novem both say, "Yes ma'am! Understood!"

Decem drives off with a sense of self and pure determination. Decem thinks to herself, "I will complete my mission, and prove that I have always been worthy of this position, let's go!"

[CHAPTER EIGHT END – ORDER OF THE CARDINAL]

Anthony says, "Hey, are you two coming or what?"

I was lost in my thoughts. I had no idea that we were going to be so close to finding where my uncle was. My mind is racing.

Anthony says, "James C'mon on man, we need to move away from the elevator doors. This entrance way has a lockdown protocol that will take effect in just a minute, so c'mon.

Just then a computerized voice says, "ELEVATOR ACCESS AREA LOCKDOWN IN 15 SECONDS. ALL PERSONNEL PROCEED TO ARRIVAL STATION "A" FOR CHECK IN CONFIRMATION AND ROOM ASSIGNMENT. LOCK DOWN IN.... 5 .... 4 .... 3 .... 2 .... 1 .... LOCK DOWN NOW IN EFFECT. PROTOCOL BURROWING PHOENIX NOW ACTIVATED. PLEASE SEE FACILITY OVERSEER FOR INSTRUCTIONS.

As the doors closed behind us I was wondering if my uncle was down here, and did he hear the security alarm go off. Jill asks, "Anthony, you said that there were other facilities connected to this one correct? If the security protocol went off, how would it affect the other facilities in conjunction with this one?"

Anthony stops in front of the bottom of the stairway and looks around for a moment. His gaze focuses on a green light lit at the top left the ceiling.

Anthony says, "You see that light right there? That light indicates that the other facilities are actively conjoined, and that travel is possible between all the facilities. There are a series of light indicators at the bottom of that, that are only lit in case access has been blocked. Once inside the evacuation chamber like the one we came in at, a computer terminal and monitor will deploy, and show available accessibility to the other underground sites. Each site has two evacuation chambers that house four lifts each that will take you to the surface. The surface evacuation chambers are only accessible from underground, so no one outside is getting in."

Jill says, "Well, that was pretty clear."

Anthony says, "Better to get it out of the way now, because that will be the least of your worries."

I say, "What do you mean the least of our worries? Would my uncle know that we were here based on what has happened?"

Anthony chuckles, "Yes, he would hear, I guess you could say, but if he is caught up in something he may not drop everything and run this way. Let's settle in first, and meet in the cafeteria area. We have supplies that will last five years down here." Anthony looks down for a moment and shakes his head. "Damn, I hope we're not down here that long." Anthony turns his gaze back towards us, and says, "Well, we shouldn't be thinking about that right now, let's get you all settled in alright."

Jill and I follow Anthony through a building that seems like a supply room. All the doors are heavily reinforced, it looks like it could handle an explosion or two. I guess safety isn't something we have to worry about here.

Anthony walks behind a counter area that has a lot of lockers. He walks up to a computer terminal, presses a button, and the keyboard descends in a downward angular fashion. It's an older terminal; a big CRT monitor shows a black screen with orange lettering. I guess this was top notch back in the early 80's – 90's. He enters a series of keystrokes.

Anthony says, "Look, if you have to get in here, the password is **NIGHTLY**. Write it down or something if you feel you will forget. This area here will provide you with all your necessary items for your living quarters, sanitized linens, and basic under-garments, including some maintenance worker's clothing. These facilities are self-contained. This entire facility is designed to keep a hundred and fifty people living comfortably for five years without the need for outside resources, so we will be good in that aspect. If you go out through the back door here on the left you will see a hallway. Just walk down, and make a right; that will take you to the living quarters. Oh if you look to your right there, in that desk there are key cards for the rooms. The cafeteria is to the left at the end of the hallway. Let's meet there in about three hours. I need a shower, and a nap. I'm sure that you two, hehe, need some time alone."

I look down for a moment, Jill walks up to me, and puts her hand on my shoulder and says, "It's been a long day, you ready to relax for a minute?" Then she whispers in my ear, "Let's go, Anthony may be helping us, but he feels like a pervert to me. Is it just me?"

I shake my head indicating that I am agreeing with her, and I say out loud, "A nap and a shower sound great!"

Anthony just smirks, and says, "What are you two whispering over there? I guess someone is only going to need one card tonight huh? Hehehe!" Jill and I both grab separate cards, and walk past Anthony in the hallway.

As we are walking Anthony shouts, "HEY, don't forget, three hours meet in the cafeteria. Your room cards will grant you access into the cafeteria, as most other community style rooms within the facility. HAVE FUN YOU TWO, HAHAHAHA!"

Jill's face turns red. She says, "Remember how I said I was going to kill him? Well, I think I still might now."

I chuckle a little bit, Jill turns and looks at me angrily, and I say, "It's alright. For now, we're safe, my uncle is most likely here somewhere, and we're together."

Jill seemed to relax at that moment. We made it to the end of the hallway, there was a sign pointing to the living quarters, and another pointing to the cafeteria. There is a key card scanner near the entrance on the left. I put the card next to the reader, and the door opens. Stale air hits my nostrils, just then the sounds of ventilation turn on.

I say, "I guess no one has been down here in sometime, or at all. Well, let's go."

Jill stops, and says, "This is my room. Hey, do you mind coming in for a minute. Honestly, I would feel a bit more comfortable if you were here while I take a shower. Do you mind?"

I just smile, and say, "I don't mind at all, and plus my room is just a few doors up anyway."

Jill says, "Thanks."

After dropping our bags and linens on the bed, I take a seat on the chair beside the desk. The rooms are spacious. The room is separated between living room, and bedroom. Jill dives into her bag, and grabs a few items, and walks into the bathroom. She turns and looks at me. She's staring for a second; it's like she wants to say something, she's smiling, but then she lets go of the smile, and says, "No funny business."

It was like the wind was knocked out of me for a second, how could she even think that, especially after what we have been through?"

I regain my composure, and say, "Hehe, don't worry I am just going to sit here and beat your high score."

Surprisingly Jill just smiles, and then closes the door. In the background you can hear the pressure of the water pipes trying to work its way through the plumbing, as if this is the first time water has been run through them. After a few moments the sound of flowing water can be heard.

Jill shouts, "James, can you crack the door for a minute? I have to ask you something." I get up and walk to the door. I have a lot of thoughts running through my head about what she could be doing behind that door, and why she wants me to open it, but this is not the time.

I crack the door open, and say, "What's up Jill, are you okay?"

Jill says, "Yes, but I need to ask you something. Do you think your uncle is here? In the worst case scenario, what do you want to do if he isn't anywhere to be found?"

I sit down in front of the door, and turn my back against the wall. I say, "What would I do? (I pause for a moment) What a question to ask me. For now, it seems that there is a high probability that he is down here. Jill, ultimately I will follow your lead, but while we are here, we gather all the intel that we can, about everything. I don't want everything that we've been through to be for nothing. We need to make the most of the situation, and we keep going. Plus, now we have another route to look at."

Jill then says, "What do you mean another route?"

I look down, and take a deep breath, and say, "Bentclay".

Jill immediately says, "No! We are not to even take that route. Your Uncle was clear on that."

I interrupt, and say, "Well, not Bentclay directly, but the people that are chasing us. I'm sure that they would have information on my Uncle. Maybe not where he is exactly, but maybe his most recent activities, or any other leads they may have. Like I said, though, I will follow your lead. You are still the more experienced out of the two of us."

There was silence, and then Jill said, "Thank you James. Hehehe, I can see my bad habits are starting to rub off on you. Never in a million years would I have thought you would suggest us to track down our hunters. However, it's not the worst idea either, but ultimately that would be our last bet, if we couldn't get anything out of here."

After that I just sat there. There was no talking for the next couple of minutes. I just listened to the running water, for some reason it was relaxing.

I started to drift off to sleep, and at that moment Jill says, "James, are you still there by the door?"

I say, "Yeah, sorry are you about to get out, I'll close the door."

Jill says, "No, I need you to do me a favor, can I trust you to do something for me?"

I tilt my head back, and say, "Yeah, what's up?"

There is a moment of silence, and then she says, "Will you scrub my back? I know this may sound out of the ordinary, but would you mind?"

I stutter, "Uh-uh, s-sure." Jill laughs, and says, "Are you okay, you're not embarrassed are you?"

I regain my composure and say, "Of course not."

I walk into the bathroom, and just then Jill says, "Catch!" The wash rag flies over the shower curtain, and I quickly catch it.

I say, "Okay, I am going to pull the curtain back."

Jill says, "okay, I'm ready."

As I pull the curtain back, Jill is sitting on a shower seat with her back to me. The steam level is pretty high, so I get down on my knees, and grab the soap that is on the ledge, apply it to the rag, and start scrubbing. She moans almost immediately, and says, "Thank you."

I say, "It's no problem."

As I get into the scrubbing I feel bumps, no wait, they are scars, and lots of them. She has been through some things. I want to ask, but I can't find myself able to speak.

Jill leans her head down, and moans again, I maintain the same level of intensity, and she says, "Oh God, yes, yes, yes. You got miracle hands James. Thank you!"

As I finish scrubbing her back, I find it hard to not to touch her scars, and for some reason I feel she is sharing herself with me. I reach out with my fingertips, and graze across the scars on her back. She shudders for a moment. I examine her whole back with my fingertips.

I can feel the tension starting to loosen up, and then Jill says, "If the scars of our past make us who we are today, I wonder what could be said about me."

I ask, "What do you mean?"

Jill just simply leans over with her elbows to her knees, and says, "James, I haven't always been a good person, and before I met your uncle, I was just a robot, doing what I was told to do, and I did it without question."

A robot? What could she mean? I stand up, and close the shower curtain and say, "Jill, whatever we've done in our past, is just that, our past. However, you can never escape the sins of your past unless you're willing to confront them, and move on from that. My father used to say something, "Those that are tied to the past can never hope to see the future." If you are still consumed with scars of your past then how can you ever hope to know that you've healed in the present to be ready for everything in the future?" I can hear Jill sobbing in the shower. "Jill are you okay? I'm sorry if I said something offensive. I don't know your life, or anything about your past. What I do know is that the person that is here before me has been kind, considerate, caring, informative, and sincere. You've had my back even when you didn't know me. It made me want to stick with you, trust, and believe in you. If you let me, I will help you mend your scars."

At that moment the shower curtain flies open and Jill tackles me to the floor. Her lips press hard against mine. Her tongue swirls around in my mouth. It was just like back in the alley, but only more so than before. I can feel her hand moving down my crotch, and she feels me. She moans deeply, and I return the favor. I move my hand down, and begin to play with her. She gasps, drawing in all the air she can. I can feel her getting wet, her body trembles, her back arches, and I can feel her pulsate. For a moment there is just this; Nothing of our mission, the people pursuing us, just this moment in time, being in synch with one another, the touch, the feel of each other giving into a moment. Just then she smiles, and puts her forehead on my forehead, and at that moment I knew this moment was over. We moved away from each other. She grabs a towel, and looks over at me.

I smiled, and said, "I'm sorry."

Jill punches me in the arm, and says, "Stupid! I was the one that threw myself at you. It's been a long time since someone seemed to actually care about me, to say those things, from the heart. Thank you. Right now I just don't want this to be this, because of the situation at hand. When it does happen, I want it to be after we've gotten to know each other more. Don't worry, I don't think that will take too long. So much has gone on over the last couple of days, but wow, how do you not have a girlfriend? You know what you're doing."

I stand up, and say, "We all have our scars Jill. Some we deal, and some that are dealt."

Jill looks at me wide eyed, and then smiles and says, "Wait here while I get dressed, and then you go and get cleaned up. I want to see if you got a bigger room than me."

I stay in the room as she gets dressed, then we walk over to my room, and as I prepare to get cleaned up Jill asks, "So the girlfriend thing, I hope that's not too personal."

I look at her, and shake my head, and say, "There is nothing more personal than what just went on a few minutes ago."

She looked at me, and her face was beet red. Jill looks back up at me, and I can tell she wants me to tell her why I am not in a relationship. I sigh, and say, "I had someone once. It was right after I started working at Parasol, without naming names; she ultimately was concerned more with what I wore, and what other people thought of me as opposed to what her real feelings truly were. We had a ton of things in common, and in the beginning everything seemed perfect, but that didn't last. I also found out she was using prescription drugs recreationally, which, well for a better word made her act crazy sometimes. I tried to change who I was because I wanted to make her happy, but that was a big mistake. She ended breaking up with me just about a year into our relationship."

Jill looked like she was in a state of shock, "How the hell did you get through all of that after putting up with her for so long."

I sat down on the bed beside her, "Jill, look we go through life with blinders on most of the time, she was the definition of that. After she left it hurt, and I had a choice, either get over it, or wallow in it. I decided that I would honor myself more if I left her memory to the wind, and because of that I improved who I was, and now here I am. Not to sound creepy or anything, but I had the confidence to talk to someone like you, actually make a decision to follow after you. I know that's because of someone like you that I am worth more than what my ex ever had seen in me." I reached out and grabbed her hand, and said, "Thank you."

Jill pulled up, and kissed me again, but this time it was different, not faking, not because we're caught up in a moment, but because I think she actually cares about me. She touches my face, smiles, and says, "Look, I'm going to go back to my room for a bit, and get some sleep. It's not that I don't want to be here, but I think if I stay and you get naked, there won't be any sleep.

I roll my head back, and say, "Oh man, I guess we'll just have to wait for the right time. Okay, I will come and get you in an hour, and we'll eat."

Jill gets up, and says, "Okay, see you in a bit." She bends back down and kisses my cheek. She waves goodbye, looks back, and walks out the door. "WHEW!" I exhaled.

I take a few minutes to cool down, get cleaned up, and changed. I am looking around at the room trying to get Jill out of my head, and I start to think about my uncle. Where can he be, and I wonder if he's here in this facility. I hope we find him soon. I drop onto the bed, and close my eyes.

It only feels like a few minutes, but I am woken up by knocking on the door. It must be Jill. I say, "Jill is that you?" There's no answer. I say, "Jill, quit playing, okay, I'm coming out." I open the door, "Huh, no one's there" I look to the right, and nothing. Just then as I am going to look to the left I notice a leg coming at me. I throw my arm up to block, but it wasn't fast enough. The kick knocked me into the door frame, and now I'm worried about Jill. With that thought I pull my arms away from my face, and I see a man in a hooded poncho. My guard is up, and the unknown assailant pulls back, it's funny, I can see him smirk. Then he gestures me to come at him. I am thinking about Jill and Anthony, and if they are all right?

I ask, "Seeing as how you've allowed me to regain my composure, who are you, and what do you want?" The man says nothing, he only gestures me to come at him. I have no choice. I pull my guard, I strafe to the right, and rush forward hoping to catch his blind spot, I change my stance mid stride to a southpaw stance, and I throw a faint hook punch to a mid-kick, it lands, no wait, he let it happen. He's spinning outward he's leading to an elbow; damn, I'm caught in his rhythm! I box up my defense around my head, the hit lands, it hurts so much. I'm on the floor; that hit was so hard. I'm staggered, but my vision is good. I'm able to regain my footing. Here he comes, he's leading in with a punch, I step into the punch, I control the rhythm now, his chest is exposed, my hits land, but he counters the second and third.

His CQC is good. If I keep getting hit like this, I am going to lose consciousness.

He laughs, and says, "Is that all you got, then the woman and older gentleman are going to die when I'm through with you. Hahahahaha, I'll take time with her too."

He's just trying to get to me, and he's doing a great job. I grit my teeth, and the assailant says, "Oh, I am getting under your skin, do you care for the woman? You have no idea who she is, do you? Well, it's time to end this, Goodnight."

His stance changes, his footwork is goofy footed. He's inching in slowly, his stance is widening, the next attack is going to be all power, but why is he telegraphing it! Everything in my body is saying, "Watch his hips", he pops off his feet and flies right at me, I step back, and draw my leg upward, and whip it downward. This is it, my last attack. The kick grazes him, and he pulls back quickly. I'm getting tired, I can't keep this up. I should have never stopped training. Just then the assailant pulled back his hood, and says, "Hi Nephew, it's been a while."

[CHAPTER NINE END – REUNION]

I'm breathing hard, damn, I feel like I'm going to pass out. I lean against the wall, I can see his face, and he looks like Dad. I gather up the word, "Dad".

Everything goes black. I hear voices, "James, James, please wake up / What do you mean that you fought him / oh man he looks messed up / How was I supposed to know he was going to pass out / We got to get him up / Just wait, give him some air, James, James."

I can see light, oh man I better turn away! Jill, I see Jill. Never mind, I'm staying. I say, "What happened? Why are you here?

Jill looks upset. She says, "You idiot, why didn't you call for help?"

I sit up, and I hear another person's voice, Anthony is talking, "C'mon man, don't rush it, take it easy.

I sit up, and I can feel Jill's hand on my back. Just then I hear another voice [FAKE ENGLISH DIALECT], "Well, well, it looks like the hero has returned to the land of the living, and no less with his damsel by his side."

I look up, and I see the unknown assailant. I say, "How did I not see this one? Uncle J, why? Never mind, I'm glad you're safe."

Jill and I stand up, and before I can get a word out Jill says, "Why, after all this time? Why couldn't you let me know where you were going? Why didn't you let me know that something was wrong? How could you just leave like that?"

Jonathan walks up towards Jill, and looks her straight in the eye, and says, "Hope. I had faith that you would find me; that you would track down the journal, and find James. I needed to get away though. I had no choice due to the nature of my situation. I'm sorry."

Jill exhales and says, "I have no idea whether I should beat you to a bloody pulp, or hug you."

I laugh and say, "Well, it's good to have you back, but I have to get something to eat, or I am going to pass out again." I move in front of my uncle and with a glare I say, "Uncle once we get through all the formalities you and I are going to have a little chat."

Anthony walks beside me, and throws my arm over his shoulder, and says, "C'mon little buddy, let's go."

We turn down the hallway, and walk towards the cafeteria. I turn my head, and I see that my uncle and Jill haven't moved. I can see Jill's back, and her arms folded facing my uncle. I turn my gaze back down the hallway, and say "I guess they have some things to work out."

Anthony shakes his head, and exhales, "Yeah man."

We make it to the cafeteria, and Anthony helps me sit in a booth area. Looking around this place feels like it is right out of the 50's & 60's. Anthony slides along the other side of the table, and says, "So, what can I get you? We pretty much have everything down here." I was thinking about Vinny's, and I wished I could go back there to eat, and then I say, "Spaghetti and Meatballs, a Pepsi, and a bottle water."

Anthony smiles, and says, "Coming right up; you know that actually sounds really good I think I'll join you. Anthony flies out of the booth, and says, "Give me about 30 minutes, everything here is freeze dried, but it'll take me a few minutes to find all the essentials."

I look up at Anthony, and say, "Man, take your time, if you could, and could you make some for the other two that haven't shown up yet?"

I can see Anthony's face look down, his eyes say everything. I should have seen it coming really. There was something more between those two than once let on. I guess I should have seen that coming.

I say, "Don't worry about it. Whatever they have, and what they have to work out, will get resolved. Let's just eat." I force a smile, and with that Anthony heads to the kitchen area. Right now I cannot afford to be sidetracked with things that I cannot control. The room becomes quiet, and I am left alone with my thoughts. I put my head down on the table, I can feel the cool metallic feeling on my skin, it's soothing, and I drift off to sleep.

The smell of meat and spices enters my nose. For a moment I forget where I'm at. I look around, and there is no one around. I can hear the sounds of music, and the banging of a pot. The smell is nice, and I decide to walk back to the kitchen. I can see Anthony cooking and singing. The music is Latin-based; the rhythm is infectious. Anthony is in his own world, lip-synching into the ladle. I lean against the side of the doorway, and close my eyes, and nod my head to the beat. At that moment Anthony sees me, and says, "Hey man, can you give me a hand?"

I say, "Sure, what do you need?"

Anthony says, "Plates, and silverware. They're all located in the storeroom to the right. Are you okay to walk?"

I smile, and say, "Yeah man, I'm all good."

I head inside the kitchen, and I see the storeroom. I am taken back by the size of the kitchen. There are vast amounts of walk-in freezers, and equipment rooms. Anthony notices I stopped in my tracks, and says, "I told you we're stocked for at least 5 years."

I say, "I can see that."

I find the room with the silverware, I grab up the plates, forks, spoons, and knives, and I head back out to the cook area, where Anthony is still jamming out to the music.

Anthony turns around, looks at me, and says, "I love Cuban music, it makes me feel alive you know? The music feels like there is a celebration happening."

I say, "So are you Cuban?"

He looks at me, and says, "A lot of people think that, but no; my Mom is American Indian, and my Father is African. I thought you knew that though."

I say, "Oh, well, I haven't seen you since I was a kid, and well you know kids don't really care about stuff like that when they're that young. It only seems to matter when you're older for some reason. I guess kids have it right. Play, eat, and sleep."

He laughs, and says, "Well us being half breeds, we usually get the best of both worlds if you get my meaning." He winks, and turns back to his cooking, and says, "Five minutes, get the table set, because it's a reunion baby!"

I smile and shout "REUNION!" I guess I scared Anthony, because his back tensed up, and his shoulders flared upward.

He turns, and says, "Whoa! YEAH, REUNION!"

Just then, I felt great, like I was revitalized. I head out and get the table ready. With the music playing in the background it feels like all my worries are fading away. I'll have to get my MP3 player out later. Without noticing my body is moving to the beat, just then I can feel someone behind me. It's Jill, and she's smiling right at me. There is a pause, I feel my body tense up for a moment, but then I remember the sense of relief and I no longer care about what may be with Jill and my Uncle. It no longer matters, I have found him. I did what I set out to do, and whatever happens from here on out will only be to my benefit, it has become so much more than me now. I smile back at her, and I know she knows.

She walks up to me, and says, "James, I'm sorry about back there, but there were some things that we needed to discuss. There are things that I'd rather you learn from me, and no one else."

As she begins to walk to the table her hand grabs mine, and I look back at her, she doesn't turn, but says, "With moves like that, we are going out after all this is over." She lets go and sits down. I can feel her tension. She has a lot on her mind, and I am sure it's her past. I won't pry, I will let her tell me whenever she's ready.

I hear a voice that says, "James" I turn my gaze back towards the cafeteria entrance, and it's my Uncle standing there. He says, "I need to talk to you right now, please follow me."

I stand up and say, "Uncle we're going to have food here in a minute, let's sit down and enjoy some food."

My uncle turns his back towards me, and says, "There is no time I need to speak with you now, with no distraction, so please follow me."

Just then Anthony comes through the doors with a cart. On it is the spaghetti sauce, a big plate of meatballs, noodles, the smell is intense and reminds me of being in a restaurant. I turn to Jill and Anthony and say, "Hey, I'll be back, don't eat all the food without me."

Anthony says, "Take your time my man. It's not every day I get to have dinner with a pretty lady."

Jill makes a frown, and she says, "Hurry up; I don't want to eat alone."

Anthony says, "Hey-y-y-y, what am I chopped liver?"

Jill and I both laugh as I walk out of the cafeteria, I can hear Anthony sighing.

As I walk through the door back into the walkway I can see my uncle in the distance. He shouts, "Hurry up, there isn't much time." What in the world is he talking about?

I say, "Uncle what are you talking about? Not enough time for what?"

He just proceeds in the same direction, as he was walking the lights in front of him were turning on as if these corridors had not been traveled through in some time. Again, I am hit with that familiar stale air that I experienced when we first arrived in the living quarters. I catch up to him, and for a while we say nothing to each other. As we traversed the area I see what appears to be classrooms through the windows on either side of the hallway.

I ask, "Uncle, what's going in, we've been walking for a while now, can you at least tell me why we're walking out this far, and what is it that you want to tell me?"

 My uncle turns and glares at me. For the first time I get to see his face. He looks like Dad sort of. I think of him, my dad, for just a moment and I wonder how he and mom are doing.

It feels like we have walked a few miles. We arrive at the end of the corridor, and the door opens up to a huge hangar area.

"Whoa!" I exclaim. "What is this?"

There are computers, and other research equipment as far as the eye can see."

My uncle turns to me, "James this is what I have to show you; the reason you've come so far, and why I couldn't tell you anything until now. The research project, "Infinite Possible" is housed and worked on here. I received government funding in the beginning, and I was also able to acquire these underground facilities as part of the deal. My disappearances for months at a time were because of the discoveries that

I've made here. Your text books may never capture the historical moments that may, no, that will transpire here, but you will bear witness to the truth of the universe here, and the secrets of this world will unravel before you, just as they have for me."

I ask, "Uncle what are you talking about? The secrets of the Universe; you sound like the videos and people on the internet that I am not supposed to believe."

My uncle takes off his poncho. What I see shocks me. His torso is riddled with cuts and bruises. He walks over to a locker, and pulls out a workers' shirt, and covers himself.

Before I can get out a word, he says, "I know that you have questions, but for now I need you to hold off on asking anything until I ask you a few things first."

I nod in acknowledgement. He points to a desk with a single monitor on it. "I need you to sit down over here for a moment." He said.

My uncle gets behind another desk, and pushes a series of buttons. One of those buttons activates a projector. The lights dim and an image is projected.

I say, "Uncle these are the images in your journal."

My uncle looks at me, and says, "Yes, but now I will take some time out to explain it to you, because if something happens to me or this journal, I know that you are the only one that will be able to record the information again if the time comes. As I said, there is more in this Universe than you know, and I am going to explain to you what I mean, and then ultimately show you. We are fighting something bigger than just Bentclay.

I say, "What do you mean show me?" My Uncle looks at me with a smile, and says, "Allow me to provide you a full explanation."

[CHAPTER TEN END – EXPLANATION]

"James before I cover the overall research let's go over some of the key terminology from the journal which will be important to this overview, and discussion. I am going to need you to hold any questions that you have until after I explain everything." The first slide is displayed on the computer screen in front of me. It's a set of definitions.

1) **POE - Point of Existence**: Within the universe we live in, as an individual entity, we make up one Point of Existence. It is the marker of our representation as part of the universal expression, The Big Bang.

2) **POE HARVESTING**: When one person harvests more than one POE

3) **MPOE – Multiverse Point of Existence / Multiple Point of Existence**: For each universe, there is a POE that represents a particular individual POE that vibrates at a particular frequency that may be unique in frequency, or almost similar.

4) **POE SHIFTING**: Similar to a quantum leap, but you transfer into the same person temporarily.

5) **Lines of Epiphany Aka Enlightenment** – There are times when the mind is active "in sync" with other POE minds. As the POE vibrates at different frequencies, there are brief times when multiple POE's sync in a timed instance.

6) **Empathetic Enlightenment** – As multiple POE's synchronize for a timed instance with an active mind (awake/consciously aware) the life lessons from the other POE all mentally sync.
NOTE Synching can be mathematically timed. Although at the moment, the knowledge of what POE sync at specific frequencies cannot be calculated to 100% accuracy.

7) **LOI – Lines of Intention**: This is defined as thoughts of actions that are taken or not taken. Actions of thought taken or not are all possible points that affect our own POE. Ultimately, this affects who we become in all facets of life.

8) **Dominant Transference / Recessive Inclusion** Depending on the personality of the POE, during

the end of one POE, as the energy flows back to the Point of Origin, if another POE shares a similar existence/frequency there is an event called POE unification

9) **POE Unification** – During this event as MPOE's are unified. There is an event that allows for traits to layer within the newly unified POE. In most instances, whichever POE is the most dominant, will retain its traits in the newly unified POE while all previous dominant traits become recessively included. This may or may not affect the overall personality.

10) **Blink Transfer** – There are instances where two similar POE's energy vibrates at the same frequency of each other which can cause a shifting between the individual's POE. The augmented shift may incur both positive and negative effects.

11) **Point of Origin / Point of Origin Return**: *(PO)* Energy can neither be created nor destroyed, just as water turns to steam due to environmental conversion. As it cools, it reverts back to its original form. This is the same for the universes created by the big bang. As the universes cool they collapse and return to the Point of Origin as part of the Universal Expression, so when all the expressed energy returns back to the Point of Origin, then the Big Bang happens again.

12) **Universal Expression** – This action defines The Big Bang.

13) **Universe Time Frequency / Concentric Universal Time / Concentric Universal Time Dilation** – While there are multiple Universes, they were not all created at the same instance. During the universal expression of the Big Bang, the universes rippled in creation. This accounts for cases known as Déjà Vu which affects all individual POE. This helps to explain the different vibrations of the parallel universes. It's not that they vibrate at different frequencies (Universal Time Frequencies) due to their unique universal fingerprint, but it's due to Concentric Universal Time Dilation.

14) **Concentric Universal Time Dilation and Latency Time Travel** – Through every universe created, time has begun to lapse, and (in every other universe created, time itself lapses) time itself causes a frequency in the universe, and once set that frequency will not end until time itself ends in that universe. By understanding and calculating the Universal Time Frequency you will be able to adjust for Concentric Universal Time Dilation and latency. With this specific type of calculation, you will be able to peer into a probable past or future. Depending if the frequencies are similar, you can alter another universe, just never the one you exist in directly.

Another POE would have to be involved to make changes happen.

15)**Universal Time Constant** – During the event of the Big Bang, while the blast was Omni directional, it does not mean the matter and energy was displaced evenly. This will account for the constant speed of time being only relative to the particular universe. In short the neighboring universe will either be years ahead of your own civilization, greatly behind, or very much corresponding.

16)**Universal Harmony** – Each universe plays out in a certain order governed by LOI. LOI is governed by the frequency of thought, and while no two universes are the same, the overall outcome may be. When another POE alters the events in another universe, which may disrupt the constant universe flow, one must be careful if treading here as there is a chance for Universal Vibrational Destabilization.

17)**Universal Vibrational Destabilization** – The reason why the individual POE of a particular universe cannot be calculated on the approximation of the lineup is due to the variance of certain universes that collapse. Instances of this may be caused by a form of Universal Stitching, aka Universal Coercion, or through a technique called, "Universal Stitch coercion".

18) **Universal Stitching Aka Universal Compression** – As an individual's entire POE end, its energy is returned to the Point of Origin, but this is its complete natural behavior.

19) **Universal Evolution** – Each time the universe resets and the Big Bang happens again, time is restarted and the universe is able to refine itself. As a living entity, the universes created become more stable on the account that fewer universes are created which increases the amount of time that the universes remain. Each time that the Big Bang happens, the Point of Origin becomes more energy efficient, and stable. The universe is learning how to control itself.

My Uncle finishes speaking, and now there is an air of silence. What the hell is all this? He stands up, wipes his eyes, smiles, and walks over to me. I stand up, and as I am about to say something he throws his finger over his lip signaling me to not to say anything. He stops across on the other side of my desk, grabs a chair and sits down. He is just staring at me, like he is the one processing, but what could he be thinking?

Just then he says, "James, if you think what I told you is unbelievable, just wait, because what I am about to tell you, will send you through the looking glass."

I sit back down and stare at him, waiting for him to say anything. My mind is reeling from the information, but I am curious about what he is going to say next.

My uncle tells me, "Okay, go back to the main screen, and click the folder on the desktop labeled **Others.**"

I click the file, and I see another power point along with a few video clips. My uncle says, "I need you to open the file that says **Indigo Children**."

The video file opens, and I see a kid sitting at a desk with a man on the side holding cards, there is no sound. On the card there are symbols, and the man seems to be asking the kid what is on the card. Judging by the gestures the kid seems to be answering correctly. Just then the video tracking seems to be messed up and cuts in and out rapidly. At that moment you see the kid rocking back and forth, just then he looks directly at the camera, and the video cuts out.

"Open the file that says **Side Camera112214**." My Uncle says.

I click the file, and the same rocking kid is there. This file has sound, so I adjust the volume so I can hear it better, and you can hear the man screaming in the background. The kid is rocking back and forth in a much more violent nature, and he speaks, "I can see you watching, I can see you all watching. You found him, and now you're WATCHING MEEEEEEEEE AHHHHHHHHHHHH!"

The video cuts out. "James, before you ask about what I am showing you, I need you to open the **Indigo Children** file. I need you to understand what you are looking at." I open up the document labeled "Indigo Children".

Indigo Children – These individual's POE are in constant alignment. Although their LOI may differ, their end path is always the same. Their beginnings and end are all stitched together. All their experiences are shared simultaneously, and are utilized right away. This leads to strong effects both mentally, and physically. Due to this process, the mind of the individual has a virtually limitless ability to access 100% of the mind, which allows for the abilities of telepathy, telekinesis, super strength / hearing / sight, and also the ability to commune with oneself, accessing the unlimited amount of POE's of itself.

I close out the file, and I see that there are three more that I haven't seen yet. I look up at my Uncle, and he says, "This incident that you've witnessed is rare. For every billion people born on this planet, there is one of these Indigo children born, and even they do not usually live past their teen years. However, there have been two reported abductions. One in India, and the other in China, but that was 20 years ago. When these children are born, they are almost immediately revered to be Gods. Their abilities awaken from the time they begin to speak full words. Some are killed out of fear, and some are taken by their respective governments for research, and finally dissection."

I say, "Uncle why are you showing me this? I understand that it's terrible what happens to these kids, but what about the other stuff? What are we doing here? What are you doing here? Why is Bentclay after us? After you? What is it that is so important to him that he has to try and capture us to get to you?"

My Uncle lowers his head for a second, and then stands up. He walks around the desk, and says, "This has everything to do with you. At first I had no idea that because of you I would have even come up with this in the first place. The research, all the years I have spent here, were because of you. I am not surprised that you have no idea what I am talking about."

I say, "What are you talking about Uncle? I mean we did some really cool things in your house, but I can't recall anything that I may have done that would have inspired you to become obsessively consumed by all of this."

My Uncle chuckles to himself, and says, "Hahaha, of course, of course, that's right you don't remember do you, but maybe this will jog your memory. The beating you took outside when you were a kid, don't you remember the little girl?" I say, "Yes, I remember her, but what about her? Don't tell me she's an Indigo Child? Don't tell me that this is what this is all about?"

My uncle says, "Yes, she is and you were the catalyst to her full awakening."

I don't know what to say. I'm at a loss for words. How could I not notice someone like that? We were friends, yes for a short time, but I would have remembered her doing things like what was seen on the video. My Uncle is just standing there waiting for me to say something. There is a question I know that I am going to have to ask, and I know that it may make me hate everything about my uncle, and I can see that he is waiting for me to speak. I stand up, and move myself away from him. I don't want his answer to set me off, and I don't want my actions to lead to something that I will regret later.

I ask, "Uncle, did you do anything to her, did you do anything to Karin?" My uncle got up, and leaned up against the wall.

His eyes gazed at me, as if he was trying to provoke me, and he said, "Yes, I did, but before you get consumed in your rage, allow me to explain, and it will become clear."

My fists clenched up, and all I could do was think about what terrible things he could have done to her. Was a life not as important as the research, and discovery? All I can do now is be patient, and wait for his explanation.

I say, "I want to know everything." My Uncle draws his back against the wall, and says, "Do you remember the fight you got into? I would imagine that you don't remember most of it due to you being knocked out for a few seconds. I was actually coming outside to look for you to let you know that the pizza I ordered arrived at the house. When I walked outside I noticed your situation. As you were getting punched and kicked while standing in front of your friend you were sucker punched across the chin, and you were knocked out. At that moment I had seen the most unbelievable thing. Your little friend tried to pick you up, she was getting hit, and just then she screamed. At that moment the most incredible thing happened, all of the kids that were surrounding you two were blown away in an instant. You regained consciousness a second or two after. I'm sure she thanked you for coming to her rescue, but she was the one that saved the day.

After your parents came to pick you up I decided that I needed to get to know my neighbors a little better. I guess the timing couldn't have been any better. Walking up to her home, I could see that things were not going well for the family. How cliché is this? Her mother was a drunk, and she had no father. I walked up to the door to introduce myself and get the little girl's name all under the guise of setting up a play date for you and her. The mother, well the mother, let's just say she had an interesting way of telling me to leave. It wasn't until later that night that I would receive a knock at the door, and how much more cliché could you get, the little girl was standing right there outside the door! I couldn't believe it. I invited her in, and offered her something to eat. She sat quietly while she ate. I just stared at her wondering if she was going to say anything at all. I can see the fresh bruises and a cigarette burn on her forearm. She was abused on a continuous basis.

I got some medicine and some bandages for her, so I could treat her wounds. I sat down beside her, and she put her arm out for me, it was like she knew.

Then she spoke, "When people see me do strange things they are curious, but afraid. How come you're not afraid Jonathan?"

Just then I knew that she was reading my thoughts. I said to her, "Should I tell you, or can't you just hear what's going on in my head?"

She said, "No, most of the time I can hear voices, but they are usually angry. Yours is quiet, there's no noise. I like it." She looks up at me, and says, "Now I can hear them, not loud, but asking. My mother hits me when she drinks, so she hits me a lot. I don't want to live with her anymore. I told her that, but she didn't like that at all, so she hit me lots of times. After she burned me, I can't remember anything but my Mom lying on the floor. I ran to see if she was okay, but she wasn't breathing. I think I did something bad, but I don't know."

She had put her hands on her face and began to cry. I asked, "What's your name?" She looks up at me with a face full of tears, and snot, and says, "Karin, my name is Karin White. Are you going to send me away? I don't want to go away with the police. They will know what I did, and then I won't be able to play with James again. Please don't send me away, I love him!"

You should have seen her James, 10 years old, and already in love. When she told me that, I called the police, I reported a disturbance under the guise of an anonymous caller with an untraceable number. So after the police arrived, the fire department and the ambulance arrived.

A few minutes later you could see the covered up stretcher, it was Karin's mom. The police came over and interviewed me. Karin hid in a closet by the front door. They asked if I had seen a little girl, and I told them no. I knew that she couldn't live with me due to the police searching the area. I had to call in a few favors from a close friend of mine, Anthony. He was able to find her records, and clear them off by scrubbing her from all census registry and vital statistic databases in the US. Basically she never existed.

The building that blew up was our first off site research facility that was on the books. The area was perfect. No one came by, there were no inspections, and there was enough room for her to run and play. She asked about you frequently over the next couple of years, but after your Father found out about me showing you how to fight, well that became impossible. I had to explain to her that seeing you was going to be a hard thing to do. I knew she understood, but she was saddened with that knowledge. It's funny though. She never gave up wanting to see you. Over the next couple years, I was able to help train her using her abilities, to allow them to cultivate, and grow.

She was a bright student, learning all that she could and training hard every day. I was so proud of her. She thought of you all the time, wanting to be like you. Yes, she has powers, but it was that characteristic of a hero, that day you put yourself in harm's way, and took on everyone surrounding her, that you demonstrated that her life was just as important as yours. That was the characteristic that you instilled in her that day. You motivated her, I think you were the one reason she didn't give up on life.

The years went by, and I was working various contracts for the government, so I was in and out all the time. Anthony was the primary caretaker for Karin when I was away. I happened to complete some projects early, and I headed back to the facility. I wanted to surprise Karin, I knew she would be in her room.

I knocked on the door, and said, "Karin, Uncle J is back". To my surprise, I heard voices, and lots of them, all talking at one time. I barged in and saw Karin staring at a mirror, and it was as if the reflection was having a conversation with her. Just then the reflection turned its head at me and pointed, then Karin turned and looked at me with a glare. The next thing I know is that I am against the wall in the hallway. I felt like I was hit by a truck.

As I was able to pull myself together Karin walked out of the room. I was stunned, she stared at me like she was surprised to see me, then she ran up to me and tackled me to the floor. "UNCLE J, YOU'RE HOME EARLY, YAY!" Karin shouted.

I was completely thrown for a loop. This made me realize that she was not in full control of her abilities, also that more research and work was going to have to be done. I needed to know what she was doing with the mirror, and why the reflection looked like it was its own entity. I won't forget that night. We had ordered some pizza, and I had also bought some ice cream, it's Karin's favorite meal combination. I remember that I couldn't hold anything down due to the hit that I had taken from Karin earlier that day. I was suffering from a concussion; I had to stay awake that night, so I decided to ask Karin about her talking to the mirror.

Karin said, "Well, I've been here by myself for a while now, and with really no one to talk to. It was about a month ago that the mirror me's and I starting talking to each other. Shortly after, I was talking to all of the me's from the mirror almost all the time. Don't worry, they're not bad, after all they are me. Now I am never alone because I have me."

I asked her how many there were of her, and she said, "Umm around 200".

Just then my mind opened up, and a new possibility of multi universe research was born. It's been a few years now since that awakening, and now we face a bigger threat than that of Bentclay alone. Because of my research and discoveries, I was able to acquire these facilities to expand on my research so that I can make changes for the betterment of humanity. Somehow Bentclay caught word of my experiments with Karin, and her training. I believe that we were compromised somehow, but I have no idea how. Right now the only thing that you need to know is that Karin is here, and she knows that you're here as well. I had to basically bribe her with her favorite pizza, and ice cream not to come over to this facility."

I stood up and said, "Uncle, are you serious? She's here? Can I see her?"

My Uncle walks over to me and puts his hand on my shoulder, and says, "No, you can't, not yet, because when she is in a heightened emotional state she loses control of herself."

Frustrated at his words, I say, "Okay, so when then?"

He smiles, and then says, "Let's try a phone conversation first. We have a phone system down here, so there is that. What do you say? Do you want to talk to your old friend?"

I look at my uncle with a big grin, and I say, "Yes, that would be awesome!"

My uncle pulls away, and his face changes to a more serious look. He says, "Look, there are some things that you will need to be aware of, there is much more to this world, to the universe that we inhabit, and there are certain dangers that you will face now that you are stepping further through the looking glass. Are you willing to accept that fact?"

I walk over to my Uncle and stare him straight in the eyes and I say, "I will have the courage to make the changes needed, and take flight because fear cannot hold me."

My Uncle smiles, and hugs me. He says, "Little buddy, I missed you. I hope that one day you can forgive me for not always being there."

Just now like when I was a kid, I can feel the light again from him. At this moment the burden of the things to come seem like a distant memory, and now I have found my missing family again, safe and sound. The embrace ends and he pats me on my head and says, "Let's go eat, I bet you're starving."

As we leave the area, and start to make our way down the hallway, I walk by a PA speaker and I hear, "**James, I've missed you**!"

[CHAPTER ELEVEN END – JOURNAL]

They drive towards the horizon; a family without expressing it vocally and without hesitation, they depend and rely on each other when the mission is on the line. Light breaks through the darkness finally and they have nearly arrived at their first destination.

"Novem, Tres, we're almost at our targeted area. Get ready!"

The computerized voice from the GPS says "**IN ONE MILE TURN RIGHT AND STAY STRAIGHT TO COORDINATES 32.6580 N, 110.0999 W. YOUR POINT OF DESTINATION WILL BE IN ONE QUARTER MILE.**" Decem looks ahead to see that the stretch of paved road ends, and now they will be travelling off road. She says, "Hold on tight because we're going off the beaten path for a bit."

As Decem veers to the right the car begins to shake, and rattle. The GPS says, "**YOUR POINT OF DESTINATION WILL BE ONE QUARTER MILE.**"

Decem holding onto the steering wheel tightly says, "Hold on everyone!" The GPS says, "**YOU HAVE ARRIVED AT YOUR DESTINATION.**"

The car comes to a stop. A cloud of dust slowly kicked up by the car settles around it. The agents sit in the car, and prepare. The sound of handgun clips being loaded breaks the eerie silence of the desert.

Agent Decem looks straight ahead, and says, "Hey, do you all see anything? I only see land. There aren't any buildings of any kind here. What kind of information did we get?" Decem put's her head on the steering wheel, and lets out a sigh of hopelessness.

Tres, and Novem look at each other, and then Novem says, "We need to get out and look. Remember, we are in a restricted area. Do you really think that what we need to find is going to be seen by the naked eye?"

Decem raises her head, and says, "Sorry, and yes, you're right, thanks Novem."

Tres opens the car door, and gets out. Tres walks in front of the car looking straight ahead and says, "Well, if we continue straight ahead, we will hit the side of the canyon. It looks to be a few thousand feet away, if we step up the pace we should reach it in about ten to fifteen minutes."

Decem, and Novem step out of the car. Decem stretches, and exhales. She walks over to Tres, and says, "Are you ready? Today is the day everything comes to fruition. Thank you for everything you taught me. Now I just ask that you believe in me."

 Tres glances over at Decem, and sees her smiling. She looks back in the direction of the canyon and says, "I have no doubts that you will be successful. Listen, and I am only going to say this once, don't be so hard on yourself. When things go wrong you must not allow that to stop you from completing your mission. You are going to be a permanent Captain one day, and you will have other agents that will depend on you to see them through on other missions. You have what is needed to be a great team leader, so believe in yourself."

Decem looks shocked and says, "Wow, how incredibly human of you to say. Hahaha, no, no, I know, I'm sorry that was rude of me to say. Thanks Agent Tres."

Novem pulls the remaining gear out of the trunk of the car, and secures the vehicle. He walks to the front with the other two agents, and says, "Agent Decem all items, with necessary inventory are packed and accounted for. Ready to head out on your order."

Decem begins to walk forward into the desert. She says, "Let's move out! We don't have time to waste!"

As the three agents walk across the desert Agent Tres says, "What are we doing, what is our next course of action?"

Decem says, "It's like Novem said, we are looking for something that's not within normal view. The canyon would be a great hiding place for military training grounds that are off the books. That is going to be our first stop."

Tres turns her gaze back to the canyon area and says, "Once we get out there we should be looking for any indication that there was some actual training out here. An old set of tire tracks, man-made trails caused by running during training exercises, anything that lets us know that military practices were going on there."

Decem says, "Yes, we cannot miss even the smallest detail." Fifteen minutes later the Agents make it to the canyon area. Agent Novem steps up toward the cliff area and looks down. He goes into one of his packs, and pulls out rock climbing gear, and says, "There is a ledge down about a hundred feet from where we are now. It looks like it leads to an entrance."

Decem says, "Good, Tres and I will stay up top, and investigate the area here. Before we go off in separate directions I need everyone to set the channel on their radios to channel five. Everyone talkie in to confirm." Decem clicks the button, and says, "Confirm radio transmission."

Tres pushes her walkie button, and says, "Confirmed."

Novem pushes his walkie button, and says, "Confirmed."

Decem says, "Okay, let's go, but be sure to check in every twenty minutes, or unless you find something sooner. Also refrain from using the Agent tag just in case we run into anyone else. It will be an awkward situation if we run into anyone out here, so let's try to not give away that we work for the government."

Novem, and Tres say, "Yes Ma'am."

Novem sets up the repelling kit and begins to descend to the bottom ledge. Tres, and Decem standby while Novem repels to the bottom. Novem looks up and yells, "I'm clear, let's make sure to stay in contact, everyone sync your times now!"

Decem looks over the ledge, and yells down, "Novem your kit is secured, let us know if you need to be pulled back up!"

Novem looks back up at Decem and throws his thumb up to acknowledge her. As Novem disappears into the entrance Tres, and Decem begin to walk in separate directions along the canyon edge.

:WALKIE Squelch: "Decem, Tres, come in, over."

Decem, and Tres stop in their tracks, and Decem says, "Go head Novem, what did you find?" There was a brief pause, and then, "De..m, res, me in ...er. Decem, Tres can you hear me?" Decem says, "Yes, we can hear you now."

Tres then says, "Did you have to come back to the entrance point?"

Novem says, "Yes, and I found something. There is a facility door here. It actually looks like a blast door, and it's strange."

Decem says, "What do you mean, please give us a full detail of everything that you see."

Novem says, "The Blast door has a small glass window, and it's thick, for sure bullet proof. What I could see through it was another entrance that has indicators of being a lift entrance. However, the door seems to only open from the inside. It looks like we are on the right trail. I am going to investigate this area some more. However, with that said communications from me will linger, over."

Decem says, "Report back in an hour from now, and that should give you enough time to find if there is another way in or not. Good work Novem!"

Novem says, "Yes ma'am. I will report back in one hour, over."

Decem lowers the walkie-talkie, and looks down at the ground and says, "Tres, no matter what we need to be there for each other. If something happens to me, I need to you to take the reins, and protect Novem."

At that moment Tres and Decem split up and walk in different directions along the canyon.

"Decem come in, over. This is Tres"

"This is Decem, go ahead Tres"

"I haven't found anything on this side. I wasn't sure if I was out of range, but it's been an hour, and I haven't heard from Novem. What should we do?"

"Tres, let's head back to the point of Novem's descent, and see if he has started to come back up. I haven't found anything either. It looks like our mission is going to start and end with that area."

"Copy that, Decem. I am making my way back to the reference point. ETA should be in fifteen minutes."

"Copy that Tres. See you then."

As the agents head back Novem prepares to start his climb back up. "Damn, the battery is dead. I'll have to make it to the top, and wait for the two to make it back." Ten minutes go by and Decem arrives first.

Decem says, "Novem are you okay? I couldn't reach you by comm?"

Novem stands up, and pulls out his walkie-talkie, and says, "The battery died. I thought that all the gear was up to date. I apologize."

Decem folds her arms in, smiles and says, "I'm just glad you're alright. Tres should be on her way here in the next five minutes or so. Did you happen to find anything while you were down there?"

Novem pulls out two electronic key cards, and hands them to Decem."Huh, it just says maintenance on here. It's weird though I know that they are electronic key cards, but there is no magnetic striping on here at all, maybe it's an internal chip setup?"

Novem reaches for the card, and holds it up. "No, there is no chip impression on the card itself, but if you look along the edging here you can see what looks like striping that follows to the back of the card to a spot where you are supposed to place a finger imprint. It looks like it's a biometric card."

Decem takes the card from Novem and says, "Let's get this scanned for prints, and see if we can preserve the biometric information."

Tres arrives and says, "I guess we're going back to the car? Good, but before we do that I need to show you all something."

The agents walk east along the canyon for ten minutes, and Tres says, "Look, see right here, tire tracks. They're not fresh, but they do lead out south. If nothing pans out with what Novem found this will be our next lead.

Decem looks up at Tres with a smile, and says, "It looks like our day is changing for the better; let's get back to the car." As the Agents neared their vehicle Decem's phone rings.

"This is Agent Decem, go ahead."

"This is Primus, what is your status Agent Decem?"

"Sir, the intel we received yielded positive results. If the target is in this area, we believe that the area searched holds access to an underground facility, and a set of tracks found by Tres also suggests that there may be other locations as well where they may be located. Everything is going according to timetable."

"Agent Decem the moment you find access into the facility I am to be informed at once. You are not to proceed any further after that."

"Sir, we are to apprehend the targets, we were not made aware of any deviation."

"Agent Decem you are not to second guess my order, because I am making the change directly. You may consider this notice. Your timetable is now twenty-four hours. Do you understand?"

"Sir, why the time change? Twenty-four hours will not allow us ample time to investigate the area."

"Agent Decem, do not question my authority, just do as you're instructed. I expect results, and as per our last conversation, if you cannot, then I will find someone who can."

"Yes sir, understood." Decem said. The phone hangs up on the other end, and Agent Decem is left with a seemingly impossible task. She turns to Novem, and Tres, and stares down at the ground for a moment. Decem is remembering Novem's concerns earlier, and tries to suppress her sense of concern from showing on her face.

Decem says softly "Tres, Novem the timetable has been moved up to 24 hours, so we have no time to waste."

"WHAT?!" Tres said. "We were on a ninety-six-hour schedule, who changed it?"

Decem lets out a big sigh, and says, "Primus. It was Agent Primus. The priority has changed as well. The capture and extraction of the targets are no longer a priority. It seems our one responsibility is to be able to gain access into the underground facilities. The moment we gain entry we are to contact Agent Primus, from there I assume we will receive new orders after entering, or be forced to pull back."

Novem walks up to Decem and says, "Decem for now let's only be concerned with getting into the facility, nothing else matters. I will not allow you to fail, so do not worry."

Novem turns to Tres, and says, "She will need all of us completely focused on this. Can you guarantee the team that you will focus on only gaining access?"

Tres' face turns red, and she snaps to. "Of course I can focus, but why is this happening?" "TRES, FOCUS!" shouted Novem. "Understood, Novem. Decem you have nothing to worry about, we will succeed. You can place your trust in me!"

Decem smiles and says, "Thanks guys. Let's get this done! Novem can you get the IR scanner; we're going to need it for the possible prints on the card. Once we get the necessary scan we'll take a deeper look at the card itself, and see if we can modify, or copy the information."

After setting up the equipment, thirty minutes go by. The Computerized voice says, "**SCAN COMPLETE.**".

Tres says, "Three sets of prints came up. Let's see here, Novem, and Decem you two are here, which means that the third one here must be the owner of the card. I am attempting to run a scan on the prints, hmm no match."

Novem says, "Well, this area is where a lot of fourth echelon training happened, so it's not surprising that the prints did not yield a match. However, that is also a good thing. It may prove that the third set of prints, mostly likely belong the owner of the card. Now all we have to do is find a maintenance access point and hope the card still works."

"Novem, how far did you get before you had to come up? I need a full detail of everything you had seen." Decem asked.

Novem says, "It was as I stated earlier, there was a blast door that has a small glass window, and is bulletproof. There was another entrance that has indicators of being a lift entrance on the other side of the blast door, however, the door seems to only open from the inside. Thinking about it now, and where I found the key cards, there might be an emergency shaft that may be accessible. I did not see a dead end, but I needed to report back, so my time down there was limited."

Decem grabs a bottle of water, and takes a drink. "Ahhhhh, that's great! Okay, so we know our first destination, but we shouldn't spend too much time there. We know that the card was for maintenance, which means that they may have just been in that particular area to repair something externally. Tres the tire tracks that you found may have belonged to them, and a service vehicle. At this point I feel that we should split up again, but I feel we will have more success sticking together with all eyes in the same area. I don't want to miss an opportunity because I failed to notice something that you two might not have, or vice versa."

Tres sits down in the passenger seat and pulls out a laptop. She says, "I need to scan the cards for any other information, also to see if they have any type of frequency that we can emulate using our phones. If the biometric information is stored on the card itself, then it should be able to be digitally recorded onto another device besides the card.

Decem says, "Wait, and give me one of the cards. I would rather something not happen to both of the cards in case a failsafe is activated rendering the cards useless."

Tres pulls one of the cards back, and hands it to Decem and she says, "That was a good call." Tres turns back to the laptop, and continues with the decryption of the card. A few minutes go by, and Tres says, "Decem I have been able to successfully isolate, and download the maintenance worker's fingerprints, and also I was able to obtain the frequency and sequencer from the card. It seems that we have all the information from the card, also a name came up -Maintenance 10. It seems generic; it's probably a security precaution, which probably means there might be a database with a name ledger."

Decem pounds the top of the car twice and says, "Good job everyone. Let's get back to it. We're going to drive the vehicle over there this time. If we can't find access to the area that Novem was in, then we follow the tracks. Tres can you send Novem and I the content you just got?"

Tres says, "Already sent, you should see two icons. One will be for the fingerprint, and the other is for the registered biometric sequencer. That one should be able to emulate the biometric frequency based on the maintenance worker."

Decem gets into the driver seat and closes the door. She leans her head back against the headrest; she exhales, and then leans forward looking straight ahead.

Her resolve is now reaffirmed, and she says, "Novem, Tres, let's go. We have a mission to complete."

At that moment Decem's phone rings; she answers, "This is Agent Decem, go ahead."

"Ah yes, Agent Decem. I'm sorry that we didn't get to talk directly last time, but I felt that I should call you."

"Who is this?" Decem said.

The man on phone chuckles, "Hehehe, if you recall, I am the Agent that was at the abandoned facility. While I still cannot identify who I am, just know that you are in danger. No doubt that Agent Primus has shortened your timeline with a new objective."

"How do you know that?"

"That my dear agent is not the question, but the question should be, what am I calling you for, surely it's not for something that you already know, now is it?"

"You have my attention. Why are you calling? What information do you wish to share?"

For a few moments there is silence, and then a gunshot *BAM! * Decem flinches. Tres and Novem both now stare intently at Decem.

"Decem what's going on?" Tres asks.

Decem covers her mouth as she can hear someone being choked on the other end of the phone. The sound of heavy breathing can be heard on the other end.

"Agent Decem put me on speaker, your whole team needs to hear this." Decem clicks over to speak.

"Okay, we're all here. Say what you've got to say."

"Of course, Decem. First, I would like to apologize for the noise in the background. It seems that I am just as expendable as you all are. This is to inform you that a team has just left from the east coast and is routed to your location. Lucky for you, they will be traveling by road due to the different stops they will have to make acquiring special equipment. This will give you roughly fifteen hours to complete your task. It seems that Primus is eliminating, or trying to eliminate anyone affiliated with this mission."

Tres says, "And how are we supposed to trust you? Primus would never eliminate, or betray his own people. That is not how we operate!"

"Oh, this must be Agent Tres. Your reputation precedes you. You've been Primus's lap dog for years, and you've completed the missions under his leadership without fail, all the while being blind to what you've really been doing. The assassinations, tactical espionage, intel gathering, and you had no idea what, or who you have really been working for all these years."

Tres is about to say something when Decem glares at her.

"Agent, what are we looking at here? Once we complete our mission, are we to be eliminated as well? Why are you helping us?" Decem asked.

"Agent Decem I am merely warning you. Regarding this mission, regardless if you complete it or not you will be ordered for elimination."

"Then what are we supposed to do?" Decem asked.

"Your only hope is to find your targets. What you decide to do from there is up to you. Perhaps you may seek their help, and warn them that their lives are now in even more danger than before. Good bye. *CLICK*

There is a silence in the vehicle. Decem says, "Look guys, from now on it's just us. I don't know what's going to happen, but we've got each other. Primus doesn't know that we've been warned I am sure of that much, so we still have accessible materials. We're going to have to take advantage of the time, and resources that we have to survive. For now, whoever our targets are, they may be our only chance for survival."

Tres interrupts and says, "If we capture the targets before the twelve-hour mark we should still be fine." Tres squeezes her legs with her hands. She shakes, and with a sense of frustration begins to cry. "Why, after all this time, my loyalty, my time, my all, our all, - why are we so expendable?

Novem how could you know? Why couldn't I see that?"

Novem looks up in his seat, and shakes his head. "The situation from the beginning arose suspicion to me. The requirements of the mission, the lack of formal contacts, all of it seemed wrong. It didn't adhere to the operating standards we're used to."

Tres looks back at Novem, with her eyes red and watery says, "But we've always had a cover of anonymity during most of our missions. That's part of our standard operating practice."

Novem exhales, and shakes his head. He says, "We've only had limited access to resources, no contact from a handler since we started this mission. The only real contact that we've had is from Primus, and the only other contact was an agent that wouldn't identify himself. You mean to tell me that you thought none of this was out of the norm? Perhaps the Agent on the phone was right about you. You blindly follow orders without thinking about what you're doing. You've become a lapdog for Primus."

Tres bursts out of the car and throws up. Decem shakes her head at Novem and says "Novem, how could you say that? I mean after all this time we've worked together? You couldn't have found an easier way to say it?"

Novem looks out to the right side of the car, and says "Perhaps. I apologize."

Decem sighs. She gets out of the car, and walks over to Tres. Tres is sitting beside her vomit looking to the sky, she says, "What are we doing, what am I doing? My whole world has just come crashing down in an instant. The order and structure that I sought for so long has been a lie."

There is a moment of silence between the two, and as Decem is about to say something Tres says, "You know, I came from a broken home. My Mom was cheating on my Dad, and he knew for a while. I could see that it bothered him a lot, but between him working two jobs, and taking care of my little brother and I, he somehow found a way to instill values into us. He was a good provider even after my Mom left us; he found a way to maintain. I'm sure there were times he wished he could give up, and just walk away from everything that reminded him of her. I remember one day he was sitting at the dinner table, and he had just got done getting off the phone with my mother and, well, as you can imagine the conversation wasn't great. There was lots of shouting, and just lots and lots of anger projected over the phone.

He caught me staring at him from around the corner of the doorway, and he said, "I'm sorry that you had to hear that. I want you to know something, even if you're not mine, you're still mine, and there is nothing in this world that I will not do for you or your brother. We're a family and we will stick together forever."

He hugged me so tightly. I could feel his warmth; it felt like he would always protect me. To my brother and I, he was our rock, our foundation. For the next year or so everything was great, but then my mother decided to show up, and she brought chaos back into our world. She came to the house with her boyfriend out of the blue, and threatened to take us away. She said she would do anything to get us back even lie about him mentally abusing the kids or worse. Needless to say my father didn't like that, and told her to leave. She said she wasn't going anywhere, and so he went to get the phone to call the police.

My little brother came downstairs, and she went to grab him. My father handed me the phone and told me to stay on while he went to save my brother. My mother's boyfriend stepped in and punched my father in the face, and then broke a wooden chair over his back. Hehehe, but my father was no weakling he got right up and grabbed and shielded my brother all the way to the kitchen with me. My father smiled and closed the door behind him. The police were on the other end of the phone, but I could only listen to, all I could do, was watch my father through the crack of the door as he fought for us. He fought off my mother and her boyfriend. He was able to get them out of the front door. He tossed the boyfriend out first and then my mother.

As he turned his back to the door all I can remember was the sound of a gunshot, and then my father falling to the ground. I ran out of the kitchen towards my father looking straight ahead where I saw my mother holding the gun that killed him. At that moment I knew our rock was gone. The piece of mind that we were a family was gone forever. From that moment on I knew what my father would have wanted me to do.

After the funeral my brother and I lived with my uncle and aunt. After I turned eighteen, I left. I made it through college, and almost immediately after graduating, I ended up with the order. I send my brother money every month, but I've only seen him once in the last ten years. I don't want that to be the last time I see him. That's not what my father would have wanted. He would have wanted me to look after him, be in his life, and protect him. It's funny, I've never once regretted my actions and decisions, but now I see that my priorities have been misplaced. I've dishonored the memory of my father, and I want to change that. I'm sorry Decem, I'm sorry if I've been cold to you, and if I never took your thoughts or feelings into consideration. I am sorry for that as well."

Tres stands up, and brushes herself off, and looks down at her vomit for a second. "Oh my god, what the hell did I eat?"

Decem smiles and says, "Whatever it was, I have some mouthwash to get the rest out." Tres and Decem laugh on the way back to the car.

Novem opens the door and stands facing Tres. "I am sorry for what I said to you. I shouldn't have said it."

Tres smiles and says, "Novem if you hadn't said it, I am not sure where my mindset would have been in the near future. I should be the one apologizing."

Novem places his hand up gesturing her to stop. "Tres you've always been loyal to the cause, but more importantly loyal to us, and while I do not express my emotions as well as Decem here, I want to say that our bond is the bond of a family, and we will look out for each other. It's us against the world, and now we need to move."

Tres, and Decem look at each other and they both smile. Novem gestures, and places his hand out. Decem and Tres place their hands on top of his. "Nos unum sumus familiae." Novem says.

Tres and Decem smile at Novem. The tension caused by the knowledge of betrayal seemingly melts away for the moment. As the sun rises into the apex of the sky the newly reformed team, stronger in their bonds, now drive to the end of the canyon to embark on a new path, and hopes of finding answers.

[CHAPTER TWELVE END – THE BOND OF THREE]

Hearing her voice now made me remember.

It was just another awesome summer vacation at my uncle's house. My friend Karin is always coming over in the morning, sometimes she climbs the tree in the backyard and gets up to my window, and sometimes she waits for me to wake up, however this day is different.

KNOCK, KNOCK

A girl's voice says, "James, are you awake?"

"Yeah I'm up." I remember looking at my alarm clock, and saying, "Karin, it's six in the morning, why are you up?"

The window opens, and Karin comes in. I sit up in bed, and wipe my eyes. She's still in her nightgown.

I asked, "Did you have a nightmare or something?"

Karin comes and sits on the other side of the bed and says, "Yeah kind of. Can I stay here with you until we go out to play?"

At this point I didn't think anything was wrong and I said, "Yeah. My uncle got donuts yesterday from Happy Giant, so when we wake up we can eat."

Karin grabs and fluffs up the other pillow, and lies close to my back. I can feel something is wrong, it's like she's in my head, I feel like crying, and I asked, "Are you okay Karin?"

She didn't say anything; she just hugged me tighter, and said, "I wish I could stay with you forever. Will you always be my friend?"

I remember the overwhelming amount of emotion flooding in the room. It had become cold, I didn't know what to do, but I said to her, "We will always be friends." The weight of the room became lighter, and warmer. I didn't know how to explain it, but I just remember falling asleep. Later that morning after eating, and getting changed Karin and I decided to play up at the top of the street. As we were playing I remember the bullies that came by that day.

Bully, "Hey kid, why are you hanging around with Starin Karin? You must not be from around here. She's weird."

Another Bully says, "Yeah, if she stares at you then bad things happen. It's because she's a witch, and her mom is a whore. My parents told me that her whole family is cursed, because no man would want a whore, or her witch daughter."

I stood up, and shouted, "GO AWAY!" The two main bullies and their friends stood in shock. They were dumbfounded. I walked up to the main bully, and told him, "Go away." Karin said, "Stop just leave us alone!"

"Hahahahaha I'm going to get you, you witch." Said the main bully.

Just then the other bully reaches out for Karin's hair, and I push his arm out of the way. "What are you doing?" I asked.

The bully looks at me and says, "We're going to have a witch hunt, and capture our first witch."

Then another bully yells out, "Burn her at the stake."

At that moment all the kids in the group were chanting, "Burn her at the stake before it's too late, Burn her at the stake before it's too late."

I got so angry, and as they were approaching us I swung my fist hitting one of the bullies. As the hit landed, I got hit across the jaw, and I blacked out. When I came to all the kids were knocked out on the ground. I guess my uncle was right about what he saw, because I didn't remember doing that.

I push the PA button, "Karin, wow after all this time, I'm glad you're safe, and well."

There was silence on the other end for a second, and then she said, "Yes, I am well. Thanks to your uncle, and Anthony for taking care of me all this time, I have no idea where I would be if Uncle J hadn't come to my rescue. James, I think about you every day, and I knew that I would see you again. I have always felt like a part of me has been with you. I always wanted to keep you safe, especially after that day when we were kids."

I look over at my uncle and say, "So Uncle J, do we have room for one more at the table?"

He looks down with his hand on his chin seemingly in deep thought to my question. He walks over to the PA and says, "Take the Red Omega shuttle. Access code is 356. James and I will be waiting for you at the receiving terminal. Hurry the food's getting cold."

CLICK The PA system turned off, and my uncle is looking at me. I know he wants to ask me something. "James what is your relationship with Jill?"

I knew this was going to come up I just didn't know when. I say, "Wow, um, okay. I like her, she's awesome, but as it stands I don't know what she wants to do. We have this whole situation going on, and so a relationship is kind of on the back burner at the moment. I am for it, but she seems to have things going on that she needs to tell me when she's ready, so I am willing to wait."

My uncle sternly says "Listen! Karin has strong feelings for you. Even though you two were kids when you separated; she still has held on to the past that you two have had. As I stated earlier, she confessed her love for you. The reason why I bring this up is because her emotions govern her abilities. I don't want a negative chain reaction of events to happen because you may not be able to return her advances, if that happens to be the case."

"Uncle, I understand. At first when you told me that she loved me, I have to admit I was shocked, but I am happy that she remembers me fondly, and that she is still a friend. If she asks me, then I will be honest with her. Let me bear that burden. You have to trust in her as well. It's okay to be prepared, but don't expect the worst out of someone because you fear that you haven't taken the calculations necessary to prevent any outcome."

My uncle smiled and said, "Indeed. You're right, but you should be prepared. Karin isn't a kid anymore, nor does she look it. I need you to be ready for that."

I say, "I understand, let's go. I'm getting hungry."

My uncle and I laugh, and he says, "Some things never change I see."

We walked off to the receiving area. As we walked nothing was said. For me frankly, it will be a chance to reconnect with the person that I had just realized had saved me all those years ago. I want to catch up, and eventually thank her. I'm curious to see how she's grown, and what she can do with her abilities. I am starting to see that what my uncle was talking about is holding true. There is a whole world that is opening up before my eyes, and now I have a front row seat. The fact that I am excited is an understatement.

Walking through the hallways for a few minutes we end up in what looked like a service tunnel. From there you hear the sounds of active machinery, and just then *BOOP* **"WELCOME TO SECTION Z. PLEASE WATCH YOUR STEP."**

The sound of the air pressure hydraulics from the doors fill the room, as the door opened up a silhouette formed, and then slowly she walked out. I understand what my uncle was talking about; she was a woman, beautiful, I was definitely awe struck.

She stops and smiles and says, "Uncle J, hi!"

He walks up to her, and says, "How did your training go?"

She smiles and says, "Thirty feet for fifteen minutes before I start getting tired."

Just then she looked over at me and said, "Can I talk to him." She smiles, and a sense of overwhelming emotions comes upon me.

"What's going on?" I say, I don't know why, but I feel like crying. What is going on?

Now I see my uncle tearing up, and he says, "Her emotions are imprinting on us. We are within proximity of her mental abilities. Karin, please focus!"

Now I feel her hugging me. The intensity of her emotions is flooding into me, so much so that I couldn't even see her move. Now I feel as if I can read her thoughts, no, she's sharing them with me. I can see everything. The childhood, I can see images of her childhood, I see her here with my uncle, a mirror, I can see multiple Karin's. They're all looking at me, surrounding me, they're all pointing at me. It's weird they have light coming from their eyes. They're walking towards me, I can't move, I hear a humming sound, it's getting louder, it hurts! Karin can you hear me, it hurts, the sound it hurts, please, it hurts. My eyes close. Now I can hear her voice, "James, James, please open your eyes, I'm here."

I open my eyes, and I'm lying down. I look up, and I can see Karin's face. I realize that she has me on her lap.

She caresses my face, and says, "James I've missed you. I have wanted to talk to you for so long. I had a couple of opportunities to, but I always chickened out."

I grab her hand, and sit up. I ask, "Where are we?"

I can see a riverbed, and feel the wind on my face. There are grassy hills as far as the eye can see. I stand up to stretch out, and I can see Karin smiling at me.

I say, "Okay, what's so funny, and what do you mean you chickened out?"

Karin stands up, and walks over to me. "James I am so glad you're here."

I ask, "What do you mean here, where is here? We were underground, now we're outside. How did you do that?".

Karin giggles and says, "Well, you're in my mind, we're still in the facility, and to answer your other question; when your Uncle took me in, he knew that I wanted to talk to you, but because of what happened between your uncle and his brother your time with him was limited. To top it off I had already run away, and your uncle hid me away. He gave me your house phone number, and I had access to a phone at the facility where I was staying, but I never could get enough courage to talk to you. I was afraid that I was going to hurt you just like I did those other kids that were picking on me, and I was even more afraid that you would think that I was weird too because of the strange things that I did afterwards. It felt like we were never destined to see each other again, well until now. You've grown up."

I smile and say, "You too. Honestly though I don't remember what happened after I got hit. All I can remember was I was alone walking home. I was so dazed that I didn't see you or any of the other kids afterwards. My uncle filled me in on the missing timeline just recently. I had no idea that you had these abilities."

Karin looked down, and smiled. She looks back up at me, and asks, "Will you take my hand, I want to show you something?"

As I reach out to grab her hand, I pause, and say "Wait, we've been in here a long time."

Just as I was about to finish my sentence she chuckles and says, "In here time is different. What are minutes in here are just milliseconds out there. When two minds synch, the connection of thoughts and actions happen on a faster level. We're basically two minds as one. You and I are perfectly synched. I have always known that you were compatible with me since we were kids. Do you remember the morning that I came in through your window early in the morning? You could feel my sadness couldn't you?"

I think back to that moment, and I remember it like it was yesterday. I say, "Yes, I remember. The room became cold when you first held on to me, and as you lay closer to my back warmth filled the room again. Hahaha, I also remember later that morning you stuffed your face with those donuts from Happy Giant."

Karin stepped back, her face turned red, and she said, "Oh my God you remember that?"

I laughed, "Ha-ha, how could I forget? You downed those donuts like you were in a donut eating contest. I understand now though. Your mom didn't always have food in the house for you. I'm sorry. I hope you don't think that I was making fun of you in a mean way?"

Karin walks up to me, the wind blows her long hair around the back of my shoulder, and she presses up against my body throwing her arms around the backside of my neck. Her eyes are peering into mine. I can feel her emotions, I can hear her thoughts, and she's waiting for me to kiss her.

I take my hands and grab the small of her back, and lean towards her ear, and I whisper, "Search my thoughts, please know that I am happy to see you, and I am sorry about breaking my promise to you, but I am here now. Things are different, and I can keep that promise of always being here for you, but I know that you know already that I care for someone. I don't want you to think that I don't care for you, it's just that, well you know."

Karin says, "Yeah, it's complicated, but for this moment, please just hold me, I missed you so much, and I don't want to let you go."

I say, "You don't have to. I am so happy to see you again." In her mind the world seemed to stand still, but then it started to slowly fade away.

"KARIN, FOCUS, Karin I need you to focus!" my uncle screamed.

I found myself embracing Karin. The amount of time that passed outside of Karin's mind was only a few seconds. She looks up at me, and smiles.

Karin says, "Sorry Uncle J, I was just overwhelmed for a moment."

I look over at my uncle, and he looks like he just got done watching the saddest movie ever."

My uncle wipes his face, and says, "It's okay. Oh man, wow! That was intense. James, are you okay?"

I look back at Karin, and I say, "Yeah, I'm fine. Let's go get something to eat."

[CHAPTER THIRTEEN END – RECONNECT AND SYNC]

As we walk back to the cafeteria, I slow down, I can feel myself trembling, and I can no longer move. My vision is starting to get hazy, and I can see Karin is running back towards me, but why is she running so slow? Oh man, I'm passing out. Karin shouts out, "James!"

I open my eyes and say, "Hey, I'm sorry I guess I just passed out from everything that happened. C'mon let's go get some food. Huh?! Why is everyone so quiet all of the sudden?"

I stand up, turn to face everyone, and "WHAT THE HELL?!" I can see Karin and my Uncle standing over my body. What is going on?

I have to get my mind right here, did I just die?

"No, you're not dead, but you need to find out why you're here, and quickly."

I jump back, and look around, "Hello, who's there?" In the distance I can see the air starting to shift, and then a voice comes through, "So, you can't see me but you can hear me, interesting. It seems that you've arrived at a transcendent point in your existence, fascinating."

I say, "Transcendent, what are you talking about? I see my body, and no one knows that I am here. I just want to know what's going on."

The air around me is becoming much denser, and it begins to penetrate my body, and just then a rush of energy courses through me. I feel like I just drank every energy drink known to man, but without the heart palpitations. The voice says, "It seems you're a natural."

"What do you mean a natural?" I ask.

"What you are feeling is your own energy that is not your own. That energy should have returned back to the Point of Origin. The harvest for you however was successful. Normally we wouldn't allow for such a thing to happen."

I turn and look around, and say, "It's like your voice is everywhere, I can't pinpoint where you are at. What do you mean that you, we don't allow for such a thing to happen? Are you talking about harvesting? Wait, what my Uncle was talking to me about earlier, so that means, wait did I die somewhere else? So my Uncle isn't crazy is he?"

The voice laughed, and then says, "Hahaha, no, and he himself has experienced this transcendent state a few times himself."

I said, "What, are you serious?" The voice says, "Yes, it seems that his life has been filled with certain levels of trauma that most people would never experience, and that is why we are allowing him to exist for the time being."

It took me a second to respond due to the voice's statement. "What do you mean for the time being? Are you all after my Uncle?"

Silence fell over the room, "Hello", I said. Still nothing, no sound, the voice seemingly gone; I look back at my body, and it seems that everyone is moving in slow motion. It's just like the time that I was mentally synched with Karin.

Just then the voice came back, "We cannot interfere for the moment due to the Indigo child's presence, so we just keep an eye on him." I say, "Did he do something wrong? Is the harvesting illegal, or wrong, because I just had it happen to me?"

"Without going too deep on the matter harvesting can be harmful to the stabilization of the universe itself. For now, you need to get back to your own plane of existence. Reach out and try and communicate with your friend, she can lead you back."

I look back at Karin, I see myself laying there on the ground, and I say, "Don't I just lay down where my body is, and I'm back?"

The voice says, "No, the link between your physical, and what we call the Essence has been severed. Reach out to her, and she will guide you back."

"I'm already here James."

I jumped back, "AHHHH, holy crap Karin you scared me."

I looked at Karin, and I see that she has a ferocious look on her face.

"Karin are you okay?" I asked.

Her hair was up on end, her eyes shown red tint that seems to flow outside of her face, and her whole body was covered in a faint blue light.

Karin says, "James get behind me now, hurry!"

I run over, and as I get behind her, she says, "You can't have him, or Uncle J, do you understand me?

I can see you, and I will teach James how to see you as well. I will not allow you to harm him."

The voice says, "Girl, if I wanted to dispatch your friend here then I could have done so moments ago. All I wanted to do was help guide him. As you can see he has harvested already, and now I will leave him in your care. Teach him, show him, what he must, and must not do. He has overwhelming potential, so I will look to you to answer all his questions. We will probably never meet again."

"Karin, what's going on?" I ask.

Karin says, "Hold on to me, I am going to bring you back, and then I will answer all your questions."

I grab onto Karin's shoulder, and a bright flash of light hits my eyes. "Karin!" I gasp.

Now I see Karin, and my Uncle staring at me. Karin is smiling at me, and says, "Are you okay James?"

I sit up, and try to stand. "Stay down, and rest for a second. You were out for a whole minute. How are you feeling?" My uncle asked.

I looked at Karin for a second and I could tell she knew that I didn't want my Uncle to know what just transpired.

I said, "I'm fine, just hungry." My uncle reaches his hand out, and helps pull me up. "Let's go little nephew, I got you." Jonathan says.

He throws my arm over his shoulder, and Karin comes along the other side, and provides support as well. I am still lightheaded from everything that happened, but now I can sense something else, it's like a light vibrating hum, or a buzz. If I just get some food in me, and then rest, I should be fine.

We make it back to the cafeteria. Jill and Anthony see us walk in, and they jump up immediately. "James!" Jill shouts out.

She comes running right up to me, and at that moment I can feel Karin pulling away from me. Jill quickly grabs onto me, and she says, "James you idiot! Why can't you stop from getting your butt kicked? I am going to be with you every step of the way from now on you hear me?!"

I smile at Jill, and say, "Thank you, but it's not what you think. For now, can I sit down? I am so hungry."

Jill nods, and Anthony says, "Hey man, your spaghetti and meatballs are ready. Jill ate three bowls already, I thought she wasn't going to stop, hehehehe, you sure can pick em."

As we walk over to the table Jill gives Anthony an icy stare, and Anthony says, "What's that look for? You eat like a bird, and there's nothing wrong with that." We sit down, and Anthony slides the bowl down towards me. The smell of the spices in the food reminds me of Vinny's, and it brings back the feeling of being back home, back before all this happened.

I start to eat, and I look up to see that no one else is eating. After slurping down the first few bites, I say, "C'mon guys, let's eat."

Karin says, "Okay, I can go for some food." Karin walks over to the table and sits across from me. She smiles, and asks, "Is it good? Anthony knows how to cook, huh?"

Just now I can feel an uncomfortable level of tension in the room. I can tell it's coming from Jill. "Jill, are you alright?"

Anthony begins to chuckle after I ask the question. Jill walks by Anthony and punches him in the arm. "Ouch, damn it Jill, you're crazy!" Anthony says.

As Jill walks to the door she turns and looks at me and says, "Take your time and eat. I will be waiting for you when you're done." She smiles quickly, and then walks out the door. There was something uncomfortable about her smile which made me want to not eat anymore, I feel like I have to go after her.

Karin reaches her hand out, and grabs mine. She looks down, and says "James, stay and eat. Like she said take your time, she will be waiting for you. You've been through so much within the last few hours; you need to take care of yourself, so please eat."

My uncle walks around the table and sits beside me and says, "She is right, now is the time to recuperate. Relax, and eat."

I look back at my bowl, and say "Thanks everyone." My Uncle, Karin, and Anthony all sit down eat. We all get caught up on things that have happened over the years. Good food with family and friends, the next hour goes by in a flash.

"James" my Uncle says. "What happened to you when you passed out?"

I figured that this conversation was going to happen. "Uncle, it was fatigue. I was just so hungry, and after everything that happened, it was just a large toll on my body."

My uncle says, "Sorry about that. This whole day has been extremely taxing on us all, and for you to go through everything you have within the past few days I guess it's understandable that you would be worn out. I have to let you know that things are going to get a little crazier, but for now, rest."

My uncle gets up, "I have a few things that I need to address, and it may take me a few hours to complete. Anthony, get James, Karen, and Jill some comm devices. I will be on frequency 1942."

Anthony says, "Way ahead of you Jonathan. I brought them with me already. I figured all these good times weren't going to last."

Jonathan says, "We should prepare for evacuation. There have been signs of activity above site Arklay. There hasn't been much movement, but the heat signatures have shown no signs of departure, so it's safe to assume they may have been following James, and Jill. Get the Evac packs ready."

Anthony looks surprised, "Are you sure, we could just shut down, and close the facility down permanently." Jonathan said, "No, if the facility is compromised then we will have to evacuate. Where there are few, there will be many, if it deals with Bentclay."

Anthony gets up, walks toward the facility storeroom entrance, and says, "I'm on it."

"James" my uncle says. "I don't want you to worry, but I do need you to be on guard if something does happen. Please I urge you to get some rest. We will talk later."

My Uncle walks out of the cafeteria, and now it's just Karin and I. She looks like she has a lot on her mind. "Karin, what's up?" I ask.

"James I want to stick with what is necessary for now, so for a while excuse me if I come across rude, okay?"

"Okay" I say.

Karin looks up, closes her eyes, and exhales. She looks back down at me; her eyes seem to see right into me.

"James, I need you to focus, we need to recreate the sync. Are you up to it?

"I'm not even worried, Karin. Honestly, I've been feeling better ever since I ate."

Karin giggles, and says "Hehehe, stop it! I'm trying to be serious here. Grab my hands, and let's re-synch."

I grab her hands, instantly I can feel her emotions again. Not as intense, and just then, I am back in the meadow area again. Karin is standing in front of me smiling, and out of nowhere she throws a punch at me.

"H-Hey, what are you doing?" I ask.

She smiles, and hops back a little bit, "Wow, I'm actually surprised you blocked that."

She looks like a boxer now. Her stance, it's perfect.

"Damn, it seems I can't escape this, but I never thought I would ever have to fight you." I said.

I gesture her to come my way. "Come on, let's go!"

She flies at me with incredible speed; her punches come in flurry of waves. She hits hard.

She screams, "OOOOHHAAHHHHHH!" She fakes a cross, and shifts her hips, and leads with a straight punch which connects to my face. The blood is coming out rapidly, and I throw my hand up to stop the fight. "Hold on." I say.

Karin leans down, and says "Move your hand." She touches my face, and then smiles, "See, there's nothing wrong."

I touch my face looking for blood, and now there is none. I ask, "What happened? I know that you cleaned my clock with that shot?"

Karin stands up, walks away, she says, "In here I am in control of everything, even the injuries you may or may not have gotten from me," Just then she had this look on her face that had me a little afraid, and it changed as quickly as it was there. "James we are going to have to train here. If you are to understand what is happening to you then you are going to need to trust me, and give me your undivided attention. It seems that we are facing two problems. One is obvious, time, and the second is you are distracted. Go and talk to Jill, okay. I know that she may be a little, um, upset that I am here with you. I can tell she wants to tell you something, so maybe it's better that we get that out of the way first.

"Karin before I leave, I need to ask you something. Are you okay?"

Karin walks over and grabs my hand, and says "Honestly, I am glad that you are here, back with me. It was hard, because you were my only real friend, and when you stopped coming by, it felt like a part of me was lost. I'm glad that your uncle took me in, and I know that it was because he was curious about me and my abilities, but it was better than anything that was going on in my life. I got to live for the first time, I never had any regrets and I have never looked back. The hope of seeing you again had been always something that gave me the strength to keep pushing through everything that I faced. It's because I loved you James, and I always will."

I came to, back in the cafeteria, and Karin was gone.

"Man, I don't think I will ever get used to that." I said. Now I have to face Jill. I don't want this to be weird, but I know this situation will be. I have so many thoughts on my mind, and I hope whatever tension she was feeling is gone now. Walking back to the dormitory area seemed to take forever, but I am here in front of Jill's door.

:KNOCK, KNOCK: "Jill are you there" I ask. There is no answer, just complete silence. "Jill I'm coming in." I walk into the room, and she's not there. Hmm, I wonder where she's at. Oh well, maybe she just needed to walk. I hope she's okay. I decide to go to my room, and as I walked in I see Jill laying on my bed asleep. I walk in and close the door. "Jill" I whisper. "I'm here."

Jill turns her head and says, "Come here and lie down with me."

I sit on the bed to take off my shoes, and then I can feel her hand on my back. "James, can I hold you, please?"

I smile and say, "sure, no problem."

As I lie down Jill curls up against my back.

She says, "James I have to tell you something, but you cannot get mad okay?"

"It's no problem, you can tell me anything." I say.

Jill clutches onto the back of my shirt. "Earlier today when you saw your Uncle and I talking; it was because of my past, and Bentclay. The groups of people that have been trailing us are members of the Order of the Cardinal, and I used to be part of them. Back when I started to first work with your uncle, I was sent in as his assistant. The position was a legitimate one. I was credentialed, and it was supposed to be a simple surveillance mission. The job was cut and dry really, just report on anything your uncle was doing. That was all. However, things took a turn about six months into my assignment, when your uncle had come back into the lab looking like he had just got out of a bar fight. It was early in the morning when he stumbled in; if I hadn't been there he would have hit the floor hard. It was then that life for me would never be the same. When your uncle came in he was covered in bruises, but as I helped him up and into a chair I witnessed his bruising recede, and disappear within moments; his breathing stabilized, and he seemed normal. I couldn't explain it, but he achieved something that Parasol Inc. had been working on for decades, a super healing factor.

When he opened his eyes, he was startled to see me, but before he could say anything something thrust the door wide open, but I couldn't see what it was. Your uncle threw me to the side, and launched forward kicking and punching something completely unseen. I was so entranced by how fast everything was happening that I let my guard down, and I was taken. All I can remember is waking up upside down in the basement of the building we were at a few days ago, retrieving the laptops. I tried my best to focus on my situation, so I could break free, but I couldn't. I was actually scared. I cried out, but there was no noise just silence. I could not escape, my wrists were bound towards the ground, and my legs were bound towards the ceiling.

The moment I thought I was alone pain seared through my body. My back was on fire, then my arms, and legs. I was cut all over, slowly, and the more I screamed, the more I could hear someone, or something laughing. It was almost as if the wind had carried the sound of a monsters laugh flowing into my ear. It never said anything, just a laugh every time it cut into me, I thought I was going to die, at that moment I had given up hope that anyone would hear me or see me. As my eyes began to close, and sound began to turn into silence, just then I saw your uncle running towards me. I thought I was hallucinating, but a while later I woke in the chair that I put your uncle in earlier. I was bandaged up, and he was sitting across from me watching, and waiting for me to come to.

"Are you alright?" Jonathan asked.

I strained to say something, "Yeah, but what the hell happened?"

Jonathan said, "I'm sorry I never wanted anyone to know anything about this, especially you. The last thing I need is you reporting this back to your bosses, but are you alright?"

I sat up, and leaned forward and said, "Even if I wanted to tell someone, I think I would have a hard time convincing myself what just happened. Don't worry, I am not going to say anything. I owe you that much for saving me, but you need to tell me what grabbed me, and what you were fighting."

Jonathan stood up, and paced around the room for a minute. "Okay, how can I put this to you in a way that you can comprehend this? Demons." He said.

"Demons?" I said.

"Yeah, but it's not what you think, it's not what anyone would really believe they really are."

"Now you are going to have to tell me everything, because I am not following." I said.

Jonathan sits back down, and lets out a deep sigh. "Okay, simply put, there are beings that live outside of universal time, and space, but they are still bound by universal law at the same time, I have coined their name as "Outsiders". However, they have the ability to drain the essence of individuals from this universe, and many others through manipulation, and coercion. These are techniques that they use and extend their overall life and power."

"Jonathan, do you even know how you're sounding? I mean, if I didn't see you fight the invisible man for myself, then I would have just left in the middle of your explanation, but even I am having a hard time digesting this. Before you say anything, I know that it's real, but you will just have to give me some time to process this. More importantly, are they going to come back?" I asked.

"No, they won't be back for some time, but it won't matter anymore. Since my last harvest I now know how to stave them off. You don't have anything to worry about."

"Ever since that moment he has been able to keep them at bay, and ward them off. Your uncle is quite impressive." Jill said.

"You know that it's hard to imagine you having a thing for my uncle." I said.

Jill chuckles, "Yes, I have to admit he's something, but I knew nothing like that would ever happen. He loves his work, and he feels it's his responsibility to protect the world with everything he has, and more."

"More?" I ask.

Jill pauses for a moment, and then says, "He is not normal by any means. The harvest, because of them, they have always tried to get him more than once, and because of that, he has had the fortune or curse of being able to harvest himself many times over. Surely you know, I can feel it on you. You're different now, the same way your uncle is. Does he know?"

I sit up from the bed and say, "No, he doesn't, or more over I haven't told him. I mean, if you can tell, then he probably knows also."

Jill sits up, and wraps her arms around me, her head lays on my back and she says, "Yeah, but he is just waiting for you, knowing that you are going to have to train, and figure out what you can do. Your uncle would talk about certain talents that are enhanced based on your potential, you just need to find out what yours is."

"Karin. She is the key. I synched with her twice, and experienced the time lapse between being in her world in comparison of being out here in our reality. If I train with her I can get a lot done in a short amount of time, and time seems to be something that we don't have, so this is a benefit I cannot look past." I said.

Jill pulls away, now I can feel the tension again, and she says, "Do you- do you have feelings for her? The fact that you can synch with her means that you have a level of trust that goes beyond the normal confines of simply just being friends; so do you?"

I look up for a minute, and remember how I felt when I saw my long lost friend, and I say "Yes, I have feelings for her, but not how you think. She was my friend when we were little. Yes, I fought for her as a kid, but she was the one that saved me. I know that I have a friend in her, someone that I can trust, someone that believes in me as much I believe in her, now more so than ever given our current circumstance."

I turn to Jill and say, "But what I told her is that I have feelings for you, and while it's been a short time knowing you, I want to explore this with you, because anything else would be a betrayal to us. I am asking you to trust me, and to trust Karin also. We are a team now, and we have to work together."

Jill leans in and kisses me, and then she says, "Go. You're right, I trust you, and I want to trust Karin too. Go find her, and learn everything you can."

I grab her hand, and say, "Before I go there is something".

Just before I could finish Jill tackles me on the bed. We begin to kiss passionately, the clothes come off at a rapid rate, and at that moment she allowed me to penetrate her; her back completely arched, and moans out of pure ecstasy. She overflows. I can feel her pouring all over me, she's about to cum, she lets out deep moan, and as I control the strokes in and out the deep moans continue until she screams out, falls on my chest, and falls into a deep sleep. I hold her there with me for a while, I know that I have to go, but even I know that would be pretty messed up if I left her now. Moreover, I want to stay here forever with her, but I have to go. I allow myself to fall asleep, it feels like a minute, but as I wake and look around I notice Jill is gone. I sit up, and I know that I have to get ready to leave. I get dressed, just as I get ready to head out I hear the bathroom door open, and I see Jill walk out.

She waves, and says, "Good luck. I'll be here when you get back."

Wow, she seems so different now, definitely a softer look almost like she's glowing.I smile and walk out the door. I feel complete, more than I have in a long time. I know what I am about to embark on will not be easy, and more than ever Karin will not go easy on me, but I have to continue to move forward if I want to protect those that are important to me. There is no turning back, this is my reality.

[CHAPTER FOURTEEN COMPLETED......... REALITY]

: VOICE OVER THE PA SYSTEM: "JAMES COME TO THE MAIN ENTRANCE AREA."

I guess someone's ready for me. I head back to the entrance where we first arrived, and I see my Uncle and Karin in the middle of the area. It looks like they brought recliners.

"Hey guys, why are there recliners here? I asked.

My uncle walks up to me, and pulls me to the side. "James, not to alarm you, but Karin went looking for you, and well, she came back looking upset. I thought you may have said something to her, but she hasn't moved from this area in the last two hours. Whatever is about to happen with the training is probably not going to be pleasant, but on the other hand, she's really fired up."

I shake my head, and my uncle laughs, and he says, "Good luck."

An uneasy feeling sets in, and I turn towards Karin, but she glances past me like she's avoiding me.

"Jonathan, please set us up." Karin says.

My uncle opens up a laptop, and sits at a table on the other side of the area. My Uncle says "Okay you two, go ahead and get comfortable. I imagine that the initial training will be done within an hour in our time. Hopefully you can hold up that long James.

Karin says, "I doubt it."

I turn and look at her, hoping that she is looking at me, so I can ask her what is wrong without asking. I can see that her arms are crossed, and her head is turned away from me. She is definitely not talking to me.

"Okay guys I am raising up the barriers just in case things get crazy, and by that I mean we're looking out for my safety." My Uncle says.

I shout out, "Wait, what do you mean?"

My uncle says, "Nothing, nothing. There is nothing to worry about. It's all precautionary. Karin ready whenever you are."

I feel Karin's hand grab mine. Just then we are back in the meadow area, but the environment feels different, there is a chill that runs down my spine. I am looking for Karin, "Karin, hello? Hey, is everything alright? Why aren't you saying anything?"

There is nothing but silence, the air feels heavy, and the sky is getting darker. As I turn looking to see if I can see her anywhere, I notice the change of the environment. The trees are dead, and the flowing grass is no more. The ground I am standing on now is exposed hard dirt, and there is a definite temperature drop.

Fine Karin, if that is the way it's going to be then I am just going to sit here and wait. It doesn't matter what I do, if you are trying to draw me out, I will just draw you in towards me. I sit, and close my eyes, and a strange feeling comes over me. I can feel myself being watched, it's almost as if my perception has extended itself a good distance from my body. The feeling is natural, so I must maintain it. I know she's there, I just don't know why she's not talking to me.

In that thought Karin's voice boomed, "James, I hope you're ready. If you think you can sense where I'm coming from then you need to think again!" I can feel my skin crawl now. The feeling is terrible, it's the feeling of someone wanting to kill, and it's emanating from everywhere. "Get ready" is whispered in my ear.

I jump back, "What the hell?" I say flustered. She's still nowhere in sight, but I know she's going to start any second. I have to stay calm. Even if I get taken down I need to have some sense of where it's coming from. I need to focus on that sense again, and expand it; I have to feel her out.

Again, there's nothing but silence. Fine I'll embrace it; I cannot allow her to freak me out, but I'm bothered by the fact that she's doing it, and a really good job of it. Calm down, just calm down and focus. I sit back down, and close my eyes. I know that feeling out this area is going to be key to her not getting the best of me. I don't know how, but I am feeling out the area in eight different directions at the same time. Was this the potential the voice from before was talking about? I still can't sense her, what the hell is she doing? I can feel myself getting frustrated, I know she's playing with me, and the feeling of not being in control of my situation is starting to get to me.

Wait, I can feel some…… **BOOM!!!** MY HEAD!!! It feels like it was about to get ripped off of my shoulders. I spend the next few seconds feeling gravel digging into my face as I bounce, and roll for the next few feet. I can feel the blood trickling down the side of my face. As I sit up and regain my composure, I try to open my eyes, but I can only open my left one.

Damn, she hits hard. I can see her walking towards me, and she says "Ha-ha, you're lucky that I didn't actually land that punch. It's impressive that you were able to even dodge it the way you did.

"I thought I was going to lose my head there. Wait, I dodged it?" I asked.

Karin stops and looks puzzled. "So, you are unaware of your own potential. It looks like your instincts saved you, because I was trying to hurt you." Just then Karin had that look from before, but this time it didn't fade away like the last time. I think she's trying to kill me.

"Karin, wait. Are you trying to kill me or something?" I ask.

Karin smiles and says, "Maybe." At that moment she comes at me with a flurry of punches. I can't see them all, and I am getting overwhelmed. I have to back up, and readjust. I am getting beat bad here. The hits are getting harder, and I'm starting to lose consciousness.

Karin says, "Where are you going? You know you can't run from me."

Damn it, she is closing on me fast. There's no use in hiding, but I have to buy some time to recover. It looks like she's right; there is no use in running. I am trying to maintain the sense while I try and create some space between us. I'm not feeling anything now. Where did she go? Is she lulling me into a false sense of security? Whatever it is, I'm taking it.

I can hear a voice in the distance. "James, where are you? What the hell is going on? James, James?" What the hell, Jill? "Jill what are you doing here?" I ask.

Jill spots me, and comes running at me full speed and says "Oh, James I was so scared." She latches onto me tightly.

I say, "I'm confused Jill. Why are you, how are you here right now?" She falls to the ground, seemingly exhausted still clutching to me tightly. She pulls me to the ground. I say, "Jill we can't be doing this now. I think Karin is trying to kill me. We have to move."

Jill looks up at me and says, "Hold me, please just hold me, I'm so scared. Don't leave me alone in this place."

I sigh, "Jill, you know that I would never leave you. Come on, we have to go."

Jill and I stand up, and she says, "Will you always protect me?"

I say, "Yes, of course I will, but first."

Just as she says, "But first, what?", I punch her right in the face.

Jill falls to the ground, and looks up at me with tears in her eyes says, "How could you do that? How could you hit me like that? What's wrong with you? Aren't you going to protect me?"

This overwhelming feeling of anger sets over me. I can feel the air swirling around me with a burning sensation that is seeping out of my body. How could she do this to me; is my only thought running through my head.

I look down at her, and she says, "James what's wrong?" I yell, "How could you do this, how could you take her form, and use her against me, huh?! Why? Is this your idea of a joke? WHAT'S WRONG WITH YOU

KARIN, AREN'T YOU SUPPOSED TO BE MY FRIEND?!?!"

Jill backs up and says, "James, it's me, it's Jill, please believe me. I move quickly towards her and rip the back of her shirt.

No scars. "DAMN YOU KARIN!" I scream. At this moment I can feel my rage building up. I lean in quickly and kick her into the air.

She screams out in pain, "Ahhhhhh!" As she's hit, and rolls down back to the ground she seems to regain her stability. Karin reverts back to her original form and stares me down.

She says, "So you could see right through me?"

I have no words, the anger that I'm building up inside is unbridled, overwhelming. I no longer see my friend; all I can see is my enemy, and say, "Let's go!"

As I lead in to charge at her I feel a great weight shifting off of me, and I am in her face. She backs up quickly looking startled, and again, I am right there in her face.

"You're mine now" I say. I throw the first punch, and it connects. Another, and another connect, it seems like each part of my body is moving on their own accord. Everything in me is going at her, and I won't let up. She is starting to hold me off. I guess the initial shock of the first couple hits must have thrown her off her game, but now she's blocking me pretty well. Just as my punch is about to connect she disappears into thin air.

I scream out, "You think that I wouldn't notice Karin?! You don't know her; you don't know anything about her! If you don't want me here, then fine, I'll leave, and I'll never see you again! I don't have time for this, do you hear me?!" I feel like I am about to explode. My gut feels heavy, my chest feels heavy, my head feels heavy; I feel like I'm breaking apart from the inside out.

And now I hear a voice, "Kill".

"What's going on, who's there?" I ask. It's just then I realize the voice is in my head. "Kill, you must kill her now, or she will kill you, then you must kill everyone, or they will kill you." The voice is deep and scratchy, but it sounds familiar. "Who are you, what do you want?" "James" Karin cries out, but I ignore her; I can only focus on the voice in my head.

"Kill them all, or they will kill you. Do this and seek us out. Find your own reality. Kill them all!" The voice says.

As the voice's words tear into me, I can hear Karin, "James, James, you got to snap out of it now!"

I see Karin in front of me, and she's getting beat up badly. "James you need to wake up!" she screams.

It's me, I'm hitting her. I'm hitting her, I can't stop, and my body isn't listening to me. "Stop, please stop, I don't want to kill her."

The attacks keep coming, and Karin can't do anything. I have to stop, I have to, "STOP!" I scream.

Just then I see Karin falling down, we're in the sky. How the hell did I get up here? I have to save her, she's not going to make it if she hits the ground, and if she dies here, I don't think it will be good for me either.

I dive towards her, and I am able to grab her before touching down to the ground. I land with her in my arms without even thinking. My body is not totally under my control, but I am able to save her. The environment changes again, and we are back in the meadow area. I look down to see if Karin is okay.

Her face seems like it's healed up, but she's not moving. "Karin are you okay? Karin?" She's not moving, "Karin, please Karin wake up. I'm so sorry, Karin!" I scream.

At that moment I see her eyes open, and close quickly. She says, "I'm okay. I just needed a moment to recover, but that was pretty close." She sits up, and says, "I'm sorry about the whole Jill thing earlier. This training requires you to tap into your potential, and the best way for that to happen is to be emotionally stimulated. It seems however that there is something awakened in you that you aren't ready for yet. Not only that, but it seems that they have been able to contact you even in here.

"Who has? Could you hear the voice too?" I ask.

Karin looks down, and hugs her knees together. She says, "The Outsiders. I knew it was them when you were talking to yourself. It seems that you have great potential, and they seem to know it."

I ask, "I thought this place was your world? How are they able to reach in here?"

Karin stands up, and turns towards me, and says "Your heart."

I was taken back, my heart? "Am I evil or something?" I ask.

Karin laughs, and says, "No silly. The potential to be good or evil affects all people on a daily basis, and you are no different. Now, are there forces out there that would use you, and try and turn you?, sure there is. At the end of the day you make the decision."

Karin walks up to me and places her hand on my chest, and says, "You are a good person, but you are a man that will choose his own path. Protect this, and guard it at all times. Your heart will always show you the way. Believe in that. I'm sorry if I hurt you. I just hope you can forgive me."

I grab her hand, and say, "What is my heart telling you now? You're my friend. Thank you for saving me again." Karin looks up at me, and smiles.

I ask, "Are you ready to leave?" Karin says, "But what about the training?" I say, "I need to talk to my uncle about something. I need to know a couple more things about the Outsiders."

Karin says, "I understand."

When I come too, I find myself on the floor about five feet away from the chair, and I see Karin pulling herself up from the floor as well. The sound the blast shield coming down is all I can hear for the moment, after the motor's stop running my uncle's voice comes in loud and clear. "James, Karin, are you okay?" He asks. My uncle runs over to help Karin, and myself up, and says "You were gone for about five minutes, but the overall observation was incredible. When you're ready, you'll have to check out the video."

[CHAPTER FIFTEEN COMPLETED...... HIDDEN POTENTIAL]

"Novem, Tres come in, status report."

"Decem, this is Tres. I have followed the tire tracks about 5 miles south, southwest of our location. It seems that there is another shaft fitting the description of what Novem discovered a few hours ago. At this point, it's safe to confirm that these are escape exits. The Main Point of Entry could be anywhere."

"Tres, good work. Listen, I need you to look for an exhaust hatch, or something that would provide ventilation, and air filtration for the underground facility below. Time is ticking down, and we need to find a way in."

"Acknowledged Decem. I will continue with the reconnaissance, and report within the next half hour."

"Copy that, Tres, out."

"Decem this is Novem."

"Go ahead Novem."

"Upon further inspection of the tunnel, it has lead me to what seems to be a maintenance tunnel, however, there doesn't seem to be any power running here. I tried the card that we discovered earlier, and it does conform to a card reader that I've located by what seems to be a door."

"Damn it! So, we have another door that won't open. It seems that they have shut the power down to all the maintenance access areas."

"Decem that may not be entirely true, allow me to present a hypothesis. While security protocols would dictate that access area such as maintenance doors be locked down when not in use, it is not out of the realm of possibility that these maintenance areas also run on a secondary power source."

"Novem what are you getting at? Are you saying there is a way in?"

"Yes, and no Decem. If this area is running on a secondary power source, it would be used to test that power is running on a complete circuit cleanly through the designated areas without using the main power."

"Decem this is Tres. Novem what are you getting at?"

"As I was saying, this would create a possible window of opportunity for us. The only thing that we need is time, and it's something that we don't have. One other problem is that we've been here for the last five to six hours, and we have no idea if the targets are watching us at this very moment. I can only assume they are aware of our presence."

"Novem this is Decem, what do you recommend?"

"My recommendation is that we continue as we are now, and make no change in our actions. If they become aware that our behavior has changed, and they are able to lock down what we are attempting then they may thwart our current objective by permanently closing off these maintenance areas. I will leave it up to you and Tres to continue to look for alternative ways to get in, as for me, I feel that waiting here is necessary, so I will remain here for the time being."

"Novem, I concur, so stay where you're at, and update us the moment anything happens."

"Acknowledged. Novem out."

Decem lets out a deep sigh, and says, "Now what? It's getting later in the day, and if Novem's hypothesis doesn't pay off we won't have a lot of time to figure something else out. All I can do is wait, and hope that Tres finds something that we can use as a Plan B. "What's your plan Bentclay; are we that expendable?" Decem thinks.

There's a silence over the airwaves for the next twenty minutes. Decem is scouring the area with her binoculars recording the area for anything that she may have missed while observing the landscape. Decem becomes startled by her cell phone ringing.

"This is Agent Decem, go ahead."

"Ahhhh, Agent Decem."

"It's you! So, you managed to get away from Bentclay's men?"

"Yes, it would seem that way, but not without cost, and that is why I am reaching out again. The bastard killed my wife, and son. I made it home a minute too late. They knew I would be there, and killed my son as soon as I made it inside my home."

Decem gasps and says, "Oh my God!"

"Agent Decem you need to warn anyone that may be aware of your current occupation that their lives are in danger. I have no idea how much help it will provide, but I hope they get a better chance than my family."

"Myself, and Novem are wards of the state, oh my God Tres."

"Goodbye Agent Decem, and good luck."

Decem gets on the walkie, and says, "Agent Tres I need you to rendezvous back here immediately!"

"Decem what's wrong, are you in trouble?"

"GET BACK HERE ON THE DOUBLE TRES, HURRY!"

Decem grabs her binoculars, and looks for Tres. "There she is. How the hell am I supposed to tell her?" Decem stutters, "O-o-oh no, Tres". The tears start rolling down her face. She sobs uncontrollably. Decem is still able to follow Tres as she backtracks on the trail. Decem lowers her binoculars, and begins to pace back and forth and mumbling, "I don't know what to do, what do I say, her poor brother, I should have told her over the phone. It's too late, she'll be here any minute."

Tres arrives back, and runs out towards Decem. Frantically Tres says "Decem what's wrong?"

Decem wipes her face, and says, "Tres you need to call your brother, he's in trouble! You need to call and warn him! Bentclay is eliminating anyone involved in this mission. The agent called again, and his wife and son were killed."

Tres places her hand on Decem's shoulder. "Decem, it's okay. The agency doesn't know about my brother, and my Aunt and Uncle are in a retirement home. I really doubt Bentclay will do anything to them. I did call my brother a little while ago though."

Decem says, "Really?" "Yeah; after our conversation I had the urge to call my brother and check in." Tres says.

Decem says excitedly, "Did you use the agency cell to call him?!"

Tres smirks, and pulls out a second cell phone. "I have this old Startek phone. No GPS, no texting, no tracking, just calls. I usually just call my Aunt, and Uncle to check in and see how everything is going from time to time. They happened to remember his number, and gave it to me. We talked for a few minutes, and I did ask him if he noticed anything weird going on, such as strange cars or people in the area. He assured me that there was nothing out of the ordinary. We ended the conversation with the mushy stuff, and I made sure that he has my number just in case."

Decem exhales, and lets out a sigh of relief, and she says, "I guess it's a good thing that I didn't use the agency phone to call you then." "

Good thing." Says Tres.

Tres walks towards to the canyon edge, and looks at the rope leading down to the cave entrance. "So, has Novem found anything yet?" Tres asked.

Decem shakes her head, "No, I should be getting a report here in the next few minutes. I hope he comes back with something." As Tres turns back towards Decem; Decem says, "Time is running out, we've got about 12 hours left, and the sun is starting to set. We know that Bentclay is in all likelihood going to betray us. I guess that's why the other agent had called to help ensure our priority is getting in, and meeting our former targets."

Tres says, "Right now you cannot get flustered. Maintain focus, and keep a cool head. We are professionals after all."

"Yeah, professionals." Decem says under her breath. "Tres, while we have this time, I need to ask you something."

Tres smiles, and says, "Yes, what is it?" Decem stands up straight and focuses on Tres and says, "You say we are professionals, and I won't argue with that, but as professionals who we are and what we do should be valued right?"

Tres says, "What are you getting at Decem?" Decem maintaining her composure says, "Why are we expendable? If we are professionals, and excel at what we do, how can our lives mean absolutely nothing to those that we take our orders from? How can someone like Bentclay have that type of power, and still be allowed to move the way he does?"

Tres stands, and begins to walk towards the cliff line, as she stops halfway towards she looks down at the ground, turns back facing Decem, smiles, and says, "Those that have power have one of two ways they can go when utilizing it. They can grow or destroy, and in either direction they choose to use it, as long it satisfies the other parties around while protecting their own self-interests then there will be no repercussion in how their power is dealt. Bentclay is no different. Look at what he is doing right now. Everything that he is trying to do; what he is trying to obtain, even I can't figure it out. No matter how brilliant that scientist is, it can't be just to get him, there is something bigger here. It feels more like a cover up, but to go to this extreme, even the organization's main office must not even know what's really going on. That would explain the limited amount of resources, and direct conversations with Bentclay only. The question is who is he really working for then?"

Decem looks stunned, "Tres do you think the organization has been compromised internally? If Bentclay is working for someone else, do you think there are other rogue operatives as well?" Tres's face lights up. "What Tres?" Decem asks.

Tres turns and faces decem with a smile, "Oh no, it's nothing. For a moment I was thinking the same thing, but something just came to me. All signs point to Bentclay as the infiltrator in the organization, I suspect that he would be the only one. Our organization is super secretive as it is, so sending more than one would compromise their infiltration purposes. No, Bentclay would only be communicating with someone from the outside, and mostly not from our own government."

Decem eyes are wide open, "Whoa, just what are we in the middle of. If that's the case, then our priority now is to get inside soon. Whatever the scientist knows will fill out that missing piece of the puzzle, and possibly ensure our survival, especially if they have the means to stop Bentclay. He wouldn't be coming full force like this unless he felt that he was in a vulnerable and compromised position."

Just then Decem gets up and runs to the cliff line. She stops, looks over the ledge, "Damn, he's not out yet." Decem pulls out her walkie and says, "Novem come in, over. Novem, please respond."

"Decem, give him a few more minutes. Novem, if nothing else is prompt, give him the allotted time. He will be back. Right now we need to figure out what we are going to do once we get inside, and once that happens, what are we going to say to the people inside that we've been pursuing?" Tres says.

Decem smiles, exhales, and says, "You're right, let's wait. While we're waiting we should probably come up with a contingency plan just in case entry is no longer a possibility. We should also consider removing the car from the vicinity, and make the cave below the cliff line our base of operations."

Tres nods in agreement. "It's a good backup plan."

CHIRP! CHIRP! "Decem, this is Novem, over." Decem grabs the walkie, "Novem what's your status?"

"It seems that the waiting paid off. The maintenance door is open."

**[CHAPTER SIXTEEN COMPLETED.........
INFILTRATION]**

"You see right here; this is the moment that the events began to dramatically change. The temperature had dropped by 10 degrees due to the air becoming much denser where you two were at." Jonathan said.

I looked over at Karin for a second, and she just smiled. "Uncle how is that even possible?" I ask.

My uncle stands and leans back against the wall. He folds his arms in looks down, and says, "The amount of energy that Karin alone uses in our own physical plane, well, depending on the ability she chooses, causes a slight variation of air density to occur."

"Wait, Uncle, what are you talking about? That would have to be some serious energy. Is man even capable of that type of output?" I ask.

Karin laughs, and says, "Stand next to me, and allow me to show you."

My uncle stands back, and Karin takes my hand. Just then I can feel my feet coming off the ground. "Can you feel the slight variation of the temperature change James?"

I can feel a slight change in the temperatures air for a moment. "Yes, I could, but it has gone back to normal just now." I said.

Karin descends back to the ground, and I have no words for a moment, I am stuck looking at Karin. I have no idea how to explain what I just witnessed.

Karin says, "I know it's a shock, but you must realize that for me there is no difference between the world in my mind, and the one where everyone else is in."

She walks over to my uncle, and the two look at each other seemingly knowing what each other is thinking. My uncle leaps back, and assumes a fighting stance. Karin's feet rise off the ground about an inch or two, and she assumes a fighting stance.

"Wait, what are you two going to do?!" I ask.

My uncle says, "James allow me to show you the possibilities of the path you are about to take."

A cold air fills the room, and then a burst of light. I'm blinded just for a moment; wait, what the hell?! These two are on the opposite sides of the room now, "Whoa!" I exclaimed.

Just then, I see my uncle fall to one knee, "Urghhhh, damn Karin you still got me."

I look over at Karin, and I see her wince as she grabs the side of her shoulder, "Uncle you should be proud of yourself. You actually connected with that one. Thank you for holding back."

My uncle turns and looks back at me; he smiles, and winks at me with his thumb up. He says, "I guess now you can go thirty-five percent."

As Karin reaches over to help my uncle up, she says, "I was going thirty-five percent already, and you were actually able to land a hit on me while holding back, so I think it's time for forty-five percent."

They stand up and look at each other, as the master instructs the student with limitless potential, the line of respect is clearly felt between these two individuals. Like a father and daughter, the bond between these two is unbreakable.

"So what do you think James?" my uncle asks.

I want to ask him all about how he got to the state that he is currently in, and how he was able to obtain his abilities.

I ask, "The Outsiders, Uncle. I need to know what they are, and why I could hear them in my head."

My uncle stops in his tracks, and yells, "KARIN! Come here! Your hand, now!"

Karin walks back to my uncle, and grabs his hand. For a few seconds their eyes are closed, and just as quickly as they closed, his eyes open. "Karin, please go find Anthony, and make the preparations just as we discussed, and thank you, I'm sorry I yelled at you."

Karin says, "It's okay. I would be a little angry too if I didn't know. I didn't mean to leave you in the dark."

The two let go of their hands, and Karin leaves without saying goodbye.

"James, now that it's just us two, let's have a conversation. I need to explain what happened. You need to know everything from the beginning."

"Uncle are you okay?" I ask. The look he gives me is the same as the times before when I was a kid hanging out with him, exploring science, and learning about life in general. I felt at ease.

He says, "James if I were to have a son I would have hoped he would be just like you, but your Father had that fortune of being able to balance out his life, and settling down."

"Thanks, but is this what you wanted to tell me, uncle?" I asked.

"No, I just wanted to let you know how proud of you I am, and if anything happens, and I never get to say it again, I have always thought highly of you, and... I..." I interrupted him, "I love you too uncle."

My Uncle clears his throat and says, "Yes, well......
Ahem....". He exhales, and regains his composure. "The Outsiders, so how do I say this. Simply put, they live outside of time and space, but still adhere to the laws of the universe before manipulation."

I ask, "Manipulation? Also, how does something live outside of time and space, and still adhere to the laws of the universe?"

My uncle chuckles and says, "Let's look at it this way; when the big bang happened, they were also part of that expression of the expansion, and expulsion of energy. How they got to stay outside of time and space is beyond me for the moment. However, my encounters have concluded that they fall under natural law, meaning they need energy to live, and they can die if a mortal wound is inflicted."

"Uncle, do you know what you're saying?" I ask.

"Yes, yes, I'm saying exactly that. We have entities that live outside of time and space, and yet still adhere to the laws of nature." My uncle says sarcastically.

I realize that the situation is even more dire than once before. "Tell me everything Uncle J."

My uncle smiles at me, "Wow, it's been a while since you've called me that. Well, let's start at the beginning shall we. James, please understand that I am going to go through this kind of quickly, so there will be no repeating. You can ask questions later, if time permits. Understood?" I nod, and then my uncle says, "Good."

Beep, Beep "Jonathan this is Anthony, come in, over". My uncle walks over to the PA system and says, "Anthony, what's the situation?"

Beep, Beep, "It's just like you thought, we've got company".

Jonathan says, "Thanks Anthony. Go ahead and prepare for extra guests, and also can you send Karin? It looks like we are going to have to speed things up down here.

Beep, Beep, "I will prepare the hospitality area, Hehehe, for them, and Karin is on her way back to you two."

My uncle turns back, and starts walking towards me. His face says it all, and now I know that things are finally going to come to a head. My uncle says, "When Karin gets here I am going to need you to focus. Not only is she going to help us out, but this will speed up the process of explaining everything while squeezing in some training."

"Damn, so we were followed." I said.

My uncle chuckled to himself and said, "Things are not what they seem, so don't worry."

Beep, Beep, "Jonathan you have another encrypted voice message."

"Put it through."

Beep, Beep, "You got it, here it is."
"Jonathan, it's Edmund. Listen, my family has been taken out. I'm not sure if they knew that I

was working with you, or it's because anyone tied to locating you is considered to be a liability due to their activity not being exactly official. Bentclay, -I believe he's closing in on you. The agents that we were using should be on the far end of the facility where you are at. They themselves will most likely be taken out by Bentclay once they announce to him that they have gained access. He has activated the Devil King squad, and they are heading to the Agent's location now. I am going into hiding until this is all over. You will find the agents resourceful, and of great help provided you can convince them to cooperate. As we discussed earlier, Agent Decem will be your best bet. If you can convince her, then the squad will undoubtedly work with you. Goodbye my friend, please continue your research, and be careful."

"Anthony, what's the situation with our guests above ground? My Uncle asked.

Beep, Beep, "They are on site ZERO, and it seems that access to the maintenance has been given. They must have found an old maintenance card, or hacked the system somehow." Anthony said.

"No, they wouldn't have been able to hack the maintenance system. There are no COM ports, or any exposed lines that they could compromise. I think you're right about the maintenance card though, somehow or another they found one. Lock area ZERO down, allow them access through the maintenance tunnels into the facility, and shut off the secondary power circuit. We are going to have a conversation with them, and hopefully without any violence."

Beep, Beep, "Understood Jonathan. It should take them about 45 minutes to get through the maintenance tunnels and into the facility. I will alert you when our guests arrive. Karin should be where you two are at in another minute or so. Good luck!"

My uncle shakes his head, and sighs. This time though, there is no smile like there usually is, he actually looks worried. "James, once Karin gets here, we will synch, and I will explain everything. James, while we are waiting I have to say you are taking all of this rather well."

I smile, and say "I'm screaming on the inside, but I am able to manage. I have to admit I feel like I am out of sorts a bit. None of this feels real. I am just processing one scenario at a time, and hopefully when this is all over I won't need therapy."

"HAHAHAHA, that's my nephew, I cannot guarantee, if you were to tell a therapist any of this the therapist would admit you into the looney bin surely, and they would throw away the key." my Uncle says.

"Uncle why are you doing this? This research, who would it benefit?" I ask.

Just then the door to the bay area opens up, and Karin walks in. "Hey, sorry it took a little while to get here. I had to let Jill know what was going on, and she is helping Anthony with the preparations as we speak."

My uncle and I just look at each other for a second, you don't have to be a mind reader to know what we are thinking, and my uncle says, "Thank you Karin, good thinking. Now you know that we are going to have company, and so I need to explain a lot of things to James, and get him trained in a short amount of time."

Karin says, "The mental router technique." I say, "What's that?" My uncle says, "Karin here acts as a router providing a gateway for two hosts to communicate."

Karin says, "Okay, let's get started, we don't have a lot of time. Sit, sit."

Karin has my uncle and I positioned facing each other a few feet apart, and then she says "Okay, you two my rate of transfer will be fifteen minutes in there for every thirty seconds out here. Our company should be here in the next thirty to thirty-five minutes, so that should give you more than enough time. This will keep the strain off me mentally and physically. Uncle J whatever environment you need I can create for you. Now you two get along and have fun."

Just as I am about to ask a question Karin's hand touches mine, and my uncle's forehead, and now we are in the facility in the spot where we were sitting at.

I see my uncle already standing up, and walking around the room. "So you want to know everything, huh?" He says.

I stand up, and look around. I say, "Wow, she doesn't miss a detail."

I hear my uncle clear his voice, and he says, "James it was about 14 years ago, that all of this happened, before that I wasn't even close to studying anything like this at all. I was researching genetics, and cloning aspects of tissue, and organs. I mean I did venture into side projects that interested me, the origin of the universe always being one in the back of my mind to be sure, but I always wanted to help people.

It was about a year before the incident with you and Karin that I had what you would call a vision. I had fallen asleep in the middle of one of my binge work sessions, and during this vision, dream I was hovering over this, what I can only describe as a huge concentric circle. At first I couldn't make out what I was staring at, but at that moment I saw streams of emanating light, making their way through, what I can only describe as the concentric circles' border lines heading to a point of origin. As I watched this, I observed more and more of these emanating lights moving towards the point of origin, but there were some that seemed to stop within the border lines, and as this event continued to happen some of these lights became brighter. As time went on I noticed a hue around the concentric circle that slowly started to dissipate. The concentric circles that were near the point of origin seemed to fade and flow back to the point of origin.

As I continued to observe the event a lightly sounding vibration began ringing in my head, then I could feel the sensation throughout my body. I was beginning to feel like there was a connection to this sensation, and what I was observing. Just then I was pulled back, and now I was observing not just one concentric circle, but many concentric circles in an omnidirectional pattern. There were multitudes of concentric circles revolving around the point of origin in all eight directions. Hundreds of concentric circles and all with the same observed events.

Just then total darkness fell, and it was followed by a voice asking a question. "Are you willing to give up everything to know everything?"

"Who's there? Where am I at?" I ask.

A long bit of silence, and then a voice much louder than before, but with an undertone of a growl, "You will come to us when you need the answers you seek. You have been shown your origins, and yet you do not understand, such a feeble mind. Come, offer your existence to us, so that all may be revealed to you."

I needed to maintain my sanity in the midst of the darkness, I knew that this entity speaking to me was a malevolent force. Everything in my being was telling me to reject this offer. At that moment the voice was gone, I fell, and then I simply woke up. I found myself on the floor as I awoke. I thought it was all just a dream, but then I could feel something near me. For a moment I thought that I was still delusional from the dream, but the bloodlust feeling emanating is something that I will never forget.

I was immediately thrown across the room by an unseen force. I pulled myself up on my mirrored dresser, and what I saw next changed me forever. I saw myself being beaten, but I couldn't see the assailant. What I thought to be my reflection was actually another me, but how could that be? As I witnessed my other self die, something happened, at that moment the emanating light that I witnessed watching the concentric circles was coming off of my other self. Something pulled me back from the mirror, and I felt my back being ripped into by something. I somehow freed myself, and ran back to the mirror. I had this overwhelming feeling to go back to the mirror, and as I did the light pressed hard on the other side of the mirror until there was an explosion.

I knew that I was hit by something, as I lay on the floor I tried to get up, and as I reached up I could see my hand covered in a dim blue light. From that point everything went blank, and once again I awoke on the floor. The lights were on, but this time the air was different. There was no bloodlust feeling, and there were no signs of an explosion at all. At first I thought it was a dream, but then all these thoughts flooded into my mind. Equations, scientific notations, theories, research details of projects that I was trying to complete, all completed and answered. It was like I had an instant download of all the answers to the problems that I was having for months. I knew then that nothing that I experienced was a dream.

For the next few months I tried to make sense of things. Besides the mental download of information, there were some other noticeable indicators, physically to be exact. I used to be asthmatic, and it wasn't until a few days after the whole incident that I realized that I hadn't used my inhaler. I used my inhaler all the time, but between what happened, and trying to maintain my work life I hadn't noticed that I didn't use it, or even need it anymore. There was no more denying it, the lights emanating that I observed within the concentric circles was the energy from individuals returning back to the point of origin, and somehow I was able to absorb it, but why?

For the next couple of days, I spent my time looking at mirrors trying to see if I could see anything out of the ordinary. I didn't find anything, and rather than continuing on like a crazy person, I decided on another course of action. I knew that I needed to somehow recreate the scenario which allowed me to see another me. I felt like I was losing my mind a bit, so I decided before I tried this, I needed to be in the same state I was in before. Before I did that I wanted to take a break and enjoy myself a little bit. There was a movie festival in town, and they were playing some classics. It was something that I didn't get a chance to do for a while, and I knew that would be the one way I could enjoy myself for a moment, and just be normal.

As the sun began to set for the evening I decided to walk there. Seeing as how I haven't had to use my inhaler for the last few days, I wanted to see how far I could actually walk without using it, giving my body a test of endurance. I made it the first mile with no problem. I was in town, and I wasn't even wheezing. I could smell all the local Mom and Pop restaurants, it was incredible. About halfway to the theater I noticed that I was being followed. It was faint, but I could definitely feel someone around me; however, when I would eye the location the presence would shift to a new location. At that moment I knew that whatever was tailing me wasn't a normal individual.

A few minutes later I made it to the theater, but I knew that I wouldn't be able to enjoy myself. At first I tried to convince myself that I was overreacting, but I knew that wasn't the case. I bought a ticket, and walked in. There was no feeling of being watched. The theater was pretty empty, which I thought was advantageous if something out of the ordinary would happen. The next four hours went off without a hitch, and I was able to relax, but the feeling was not to last. As I was walking back to my residence the feeling of being followed happened again. This time I felt like I was on edge, and I was forced to be on the defensive.

I stopped once I was out of the city limits. "Come out!" I said. "I don't know what you want, but you need to stop following me."

I heard a laugh from behind me, it was a woman. I turned to see who it was, but all I could see were the town buildings. "Huh, I guess it was nothing." I said.

As I turned around I am introduced to a knife placed into my abdomen. I looked down, and I saw my blood riding along the blade. I looked up and saw my assailant.

She smiled at me, and said "Hello Jonathan." I can feel her twist the knife. Panic and shock take over, and I cannot move. "Did you really think you could get away with what you did back there? Return what doesn't belong to you, and die."

I am able to pull away. "What, what are you doing? I haven't taken anything." I ask.

The woman walks towards me and says, "I must finish you off quickly, before you can recover."

I thought to myself, "Recover; what is she talking about?"

Just then I could feel the blood stop flowing out of my body. I continue to back up, and just as I am working on recovering, she charges at me at a high rate of speed. I feel like I cannot react fast enough, but my body just moved on its own, and the knife just grazed me.

She gnashes her teeth in anger, "Damn it! I took too long, and now it appears you have some fight in you."

I shake my head and say, "No fight, I just want to know why you're trying to kill me for something that I didn't take."

The woman stops, and looks confused. She says, "For someone of your intelligence you are stupid. What you took is of you, but not you, it must return to the point of origin. You have the shine of someone that has harvested.

"The shine?" I asked.

Just then, I realized what she was talking about. The other me that died, and the explosion, I get it now.

"So I, what you call harvested, took my others' energy that was supposed to return to the point of origin?"

She says, "Yes, but you and your kind are not ready for such unification. Such petty minds, no, you are not ready, and you have disrupted the balance. Time to die doctor!"

At that moment I could feel my body take over; I could see her slowing down, as if my mind was running faster and I was able to analyze the whole situation. I could see where her next move was going to be, and so I moved. The knife hit me, but only grazed me, and again she comes at me, but with more intensity this time. She is able to get behind me as I try to anticipate her next movement. Instead of letting my body move on its own she is able to cut my back. It's time to go back to square one. She comes at me again, swinging, but this time it's different, and I am able to see her movements clear as day. I have to finish this. She lunges in, and I grab her hand, and work the knife out.

"NO!" she says.

As I am still in motion I am able to rotate around her, and place the knife in the back of her leg.

She screams, "Arrrrrghh!"

As she limps away from me, I ask, "Who are you? Who do you work for, and why are you after me? This harvesting wasn't intentional, so where were you all when I was being attacked, and where were you when my other self was getting killed? How many other people have had to experience that type of traumatic experience, but only to die at the hands of someone like you? What gives you the right? Give me a reason not to end your life here and now?!"

She pulls the knife out, and drops to the ground on one knee, and says, "It is what we do with those that harvest. You have broken the rules, and now you must return what belongs to the origin."

I stepped back for a moment to collect my thoughts. I knew what I had to ask. "How can I have broken the rules, if what is part of me is returned to me?"

She looks up at me and says, "Are you going to kill me here? Why are you stalling by asking questions you have no need to know about?"

For some reason I couldn't explain, I was overcome with emotion for my assailant, so I knelt down and said, "Because I want to learn, and understand, because I was almost killed by something that I couldn't see."

Her eyes brightened with a curious look, "Explain yourself, I have already healed, but you have piqued my interest. I promise that I will not attempt to attack you."

I exhaled, and started from the beginning. I told her about the dream that I was having with the concentric circles, emanating lights, and the voice in the darkness. She stood up and began to walk around, she was muttering something, but then she turned to me and said, "So the time has begun for your kind to finally unify within yourselves."

She chuckled, and then said, "I cannot reveal everything to you, but I can say this without repercussion. Your kind was the first, and now it is the last within the universe to experience what is about to happen. I had no idea that I would be the one to report this. You have no idea how many eons have gone by with no awakening from someone who was not born awoken."

"What do you mean awoken?" I asked.

As I finished asking the question she quickly turned and placed her hands on the sides of my face. Instantly I was in the sky. I looked down and I fell almost immediately, but I did not descend. I was standing on something that was not physically tangible, but I could see the earth below me. As I regained my composure I could hear laughter from behind.

The woman assailant was laughing, and she says, "Oh my, you really are just a child. Your bodily expression, (she continues on by laughing) hahahahaha, oh my!"

I turn and walk towards her, "I'm glad to see that this is funny to you, but would you mind explaining yourself please?"

"Yes, certainly, but please allow me to regain my composure here." She said.

She began to walk around the area, and as she did the environment changed. Now we were above the earth past the exosphere. The site in and of itself was beautifully inspiring.

As I was taken with the view, she says, "By the time we finish this conversation, it will only be as if a few seconds have passed. The way you perceive time here will be different, but I have digressed from the main point here. I need you to hold off all questions, as there will be no answers. All I can do is give you a warning, and even in that I am sure that I am breaking protocol."

I nod, and say, "I understand, thank you."

She smiles, and says, "The entity that spoke to you, was trying to coerce you into giving something that does not belong to them, which would grant them more power by augmenting the universe to their will. We cannot allow this. What you have experienced is something that our, how shall I say this, order tries to prohibit. We work to maintain universal stability. However, what has happened to you I believe is not natural to our line of work, and your case is special."

She pauses for a second, as if apprehensive at what she was about to say. "The entity that you were almost killed by, we call them Outsiders. They are like us, but they have a different agenda for the universe. They believe that they are the masters, and because they live outside of space and time they can take and shape the universe in any way they see fit. They coerce individuals into offering themselves to them by exchange of desires. By doing this, they cause a harvest rift by obtaining a possible existence, and instilling that life or lives into that plane of existence into the individual. This creates a destabilization in the universal fabric which allows them to draw out the individual's life force for their own purposes. We call this universal stitch coercion. As you can see, you have completely healed from a nearly mortal stab wound, and yet you are unaffected, and probably almost forgot that you could have died. Due to what you are experiencing with your healing ability, and probably noticeable mental abilities, such as perception and other cognitive abilities, this may not sound like a terrible thing. However, it would be in the wrong hands and your kind up until just a few days ago, wasn't ready. Your dream wasn't what you would call a dream. You have actually viewed the universal construct which is why you were detected by the Outsiders, and almost killed. Your essence would be considered evolved, and because of that, and the simple fact that you've harvested, you will probably be sought out by them."

Her demeanor changes, she walks over to me, and places her hand in mine. "I'm sorry but from here on this is all I can do for you."

For a moment my mind is opened, massive amounts of information regarding fighting techniques and languages I've never heard before, but somehow can understand, all just seem to flow in.

There was something else, something affecting my senses; I could hear the assailant's voice. "I will talk to my superiors about your current circumstance, but I am not sure how long it will be until I can give you the answers to all the questions that you may have. Good luck."

As she smiles at me everything fades to white, and I am back right outside the city limits. I turn to look around to see if I see her around anywhere, but there is nothing. I look at the ground to see if the blood stains from her stab wound are still on the ground. There is nothing at all. It was as if this whole instance never happened, but I know it did.

The information that she passed on is strongly ingrained in my mind. My body feels a hundred percent better. I needed to try something; there was a move in my head that I wanted to try. I looked around to make sure there was no one driving, or walking by. I set into a pose that closely emulated that of a Wushu stance. I took a step forward and spun in a seven hundred and twenty degree turn, and finished the movement with an inward snap kick that landed on the same foot.

I was so high in the air that when I landed I almost fell forward. "Holy, what the?!" I thought.

From there I decided to perfect my fighting style, so that I could protect myself from the Outsiders. My assailant, who had become my savior, had given me the tools to survive. I would not squander them.

Over the course of the next year I found myself being followed and attacked. The frequency of the attacks became easier to anticipate. In the beginning I wasn't able to sleep, but luckily I was full of energy. I could go days, or even a week without sleep, and be able to rest for half the time, and wake up refreshed. As the next two years went on my perception increased, and I could start to see the images of the Outsiders in more detail. It wasn't until years later that I was heading back to the facility where Jill and I worked at. It was there I was almost killed again.

I went to the main lobby, and my head started to hurt. There was a vibration ringing in my ear, it progressively became louder to the point that it halted me in my tracks for a minute. As I looked up I could see my reflection in the mirrored ceiling, and it was being attacked. After all this time they are still coming after me. I looked around and there was nothing around me. The ringing from the vibration was becoming much louder, and it had distorted my vision. As I watched my reflection, I noticed that the ceiling became like water, and just then I could see the Outsider that was attacking my reflection. It looked right at me as if it knew that I could see it. My reflective side punched the Outsider while it was distracted, and just then the Outsider stabbed and killed my reflective counterpart. The Outsider moved into the position of emanating light, but the light moved around it. This time the light did not explode through like before; it seamlessly flowed through the water-like reflection and infused itself to my body.

The feeling was immediately rejuvenating, and the timing could not have been better as the Outsider itself jumped through, and immediately began attacking. This was the first time that I could see the image in its entirety. Arms, torso, legs, the being was about seven feet tall. It was fast, and even with the ability to slow the area around me, it was coming at me with a high level of speed.

I was hit and taken to the ground. It began stomping on my back, "Arrrgggh" I screamed out.

I was thrown to the other side of the floor. I got back up and continued to dodge the punches, and kicks thrown at me. It went in to grab me, but I was able to avoid capture, and counter with an uppercut. The hit was so hard that I sent the Outsider flying. I had forgotten that I just assimilated another portion of the essence, and harvested again, so it wasn't hard to imagine that I was stronger. I wasn't recovering as fast as before.

I hit the elevator button and before getting on I looked around to see if I could see it. The Outsider was gone. As I got on the elevator, I found it harder to breathe. This wasn't an asthmatic attack; it was mainly from my back being stomped on. I made it to my floor, and walked through the room. I noticed Jill there, but I was too messed up at the time to even speak.

Jill caught me just in time, and placed me on a chair.
While she was looking me over the door to the room
was kicked in, and I could see the intruder. It was the
same Outsider that I was fighting downstairs in the
foyer area. I pushed Jill to the side, and as I was
fighting it off I noticed that another Outsider had
grabbed Jill, and taken her out of the room. "Damn it,
no! Jill!" I yelled.

"Hehehe, focus on the fight here and now, otherwise
you're DEAD!" the Outsider said.

I had no time for this and I needed to finish it quickly,
because Jill's life was in danger, and I knew that they
were going to use her, ultimately, to get to me.

I was becoming angry and I was losing myself in the
fight. I could feel the bloodlust building up inside, all I
was thinking about was the fight, and ending this
Outsiders life. In the back of my mind, I could hear a
woman's voice, "Do not give in. Fight and live, protect
the girl."

I knew who it was, and it snapped me out of my
bloodlust fever. "I thought you weren't going to help me
anymore." I said.

"What are you talking about?" The Outsider asked.

The momentary distraction allowed me to release my
special move, "Kami no dorangonkikku!" I shouted. The
kick landed and snapped its neck. I didn't have time to

savor the victory, as Jill's life was in the balance. Because of the new essence, I was able to immediately feel out the presence of the Outsider.

The Outsider was already in the basement. I made it to the stairway area. I had this overwhelming urge to jump through the stairway opening that lead straight down. Listening to my body I went with it, and jumped feet first down ten flights of stairs. Coming to the last floor the side wall was longer on the left and so I was able to break the velocity, and reduce the speed of the drop by kicking off, and landing directly in the basement structure. I could hear Jill screaming, she was close. I ran through the doorway into the parking lot, and found her strung upside down, "Jill!" I screamed out.

I was attacked immediately, but this Outsider was nowhere near as strong as the one I fought earlier. I was able to render the Outsider unconscious with a few punches to the head. I ran over to Jill, cut her down from her constraints, and took her back up to the office. As I was bandaging her up I saw that her back and her legs were torn into. Somehow she managed to stay alive. Up to this point I imagine she told you the rest already."

I nodded, and said, "Yes."

My uncle said, "Good." He looks up, shouts "Karin can you change the area to a more suitable training area.

Karin voice echoes, "Yes."

Instantly we are in a Dojo. The Dojo is top covered, but all sides are exposed to nature. A warm breeze flows in, and the sounds of a Koi pond and chirping birds fill the background. I see my uncle in a karate gi, and then he smiles, and looks at me. I raise my hands, and notice that I am in a gi now as well.

"Karin, I need a time check." My uncle yells out. Karin says, "Twenty minutes out here. Anthony just reported in, and he was able find the agents, and they are on their way here. They are closing onto the Arklay site a bit faster than anticipated. Anthony has locked down that site, and also your office has been secured. All data has been uploaded to the computers here within Section Z, and wiped from that immediate area."

My uncle says, "Thanks Karin. We'll be five more minutes your time."

My uncle turns towards to me, and says, "Let's get started. Let's see what you remember." For the next half hour, we went over the basics of what he taught me as a kid.

"Hmm, it seems that you've developed as a fighter. Did you study other martial arts after my instruction?" My uncle asked.

I said, "Yes. I trained at local schools for the past 10 years, jujitsu, and different variations of karate until I was out of college. I didn't stop training; I just didn't pursue anymore formalized training after college."

My uncle has a stern look on his face, he begins to walk back and forth, and turns to look at me. "Listen, James I am going to teach you a technique that will allow you to push your muscle usage past the normal capacity range. Based on what I have observed, from our little skirmish a little while ago, and now going over the basics with you, I can see that you are ready for a five to seven percent increase in your muscle usage capacity without exerting yourself, or doing bodily harm internally. It may not sound like a lot now, but this technique that I am teaching you will evolve with you over time. Thanks to the harvesting that you went through, your body is more than capable of handling this technique. Plus, this will be easier for you to get adjusted to the technique."

Right now I am surprised, but I shouldn't be. After everything that I've been through within this past week, I shouldn't be shocked to learn that there are newer things that I can do physically.

I say, "Uncle, are you saying that I will be able to move faster, and hit harder?"

He says, "Yes, but not only that. You are able to perceive things faster, and as the ability continues to evolve you will be able to react in real time. Meaning that, the training that you are starting today will allow for your body to move almost on its own. Whether you've thought about it or not, you've evolved."

Honestly, I haven't thought about that at all. "Uncle, just taking all this in minute by minute, I actually haven't had the time to sit back and reflect on everything that has happened to me." I say.

"It's understandable, and with that, let's continue; we don't have much time. James please take a minute to clear your mind and watch, okay." my uncle says.

He grabs three wooden training dummies, and sets them in an angled pattern ten feet from each other. He walks back towards the first dummy, and stands about the same ten-foot distance from the first one, and then he says, "James, step up about five feet, and move to your left about a foot; perfect, thank you. Now focus on my movement. I need you to pay attention to my leg placement. I am going to try and slow it down for you as best as I can."

At that moment my uncle closes his eyes, and exhales. He's focused on controlling his breathing, and just then he moves to the first dummy in a flash! I almost didn't see his feet move at all. Now he's at the second dummy, now the third, and, in front of me.

"Ooof! Wow, I could barely keep up with your movements!" I say surprised.

My uncle extends his hand, and helps me up. "Do you think you got it?" He asks.

"Let me try. It wasn't so much your feet that moved, but more of the twitch in your legs."

My uncle extends his arm, and says, "Please demonstrate." I take my stance which emulates my uncle's. As I begin to think of moving Karin says, "Uncle J, Anthony just called over the PA, company is here."

My uncle says, "Okay Karin bring us back." He looks at me for a second, smiles, and says, "This brought back some good memories of the good old days".

I smile back, and I say, "Yeah, definitely."

As my uncle starts to vanish I wonder what's going to happen once we get back to the real world. I blink, and next thing I see is Karin smiling at me. "Are you okay?" she asks.

"Yeah, I'm fine. I feel like I've been gone a while."

She just continues to smile, and says, "Well, welcome back."

She stands up, and helps me up. My uncle walks over to the PA system, and says, "Anthony, are they in the Arklay facility?"

BEEP, BEEP, "Yes, they are there, and we've already dispensed with the introductions. Long and short of it is, they want to see you right away."

My uncle pulls away from the PA for a second, and pushes a series of buttons, and says, "This is Doctor Edwards. May I have the names of our new guests?"

There is a silence on the other end for about thirty seconds. "Can you hear me? This is Agent Decem. I am accompanied by Agent Novem, and Agent Tres."

My uncle says, "Are we setting plates for you, or are we keeping you prisoner forever?"

Agent Decem replies, "We don't have time for this, Bentclay is on his way to this location, and once he gets what he needs from you, he is going to kill everyone here."

My uncle pauses for a moment, and then says, "So are you looking for our help? You know that once you side with us against Bentclay, returning to the Order is out of the question for you, right?"

Another long pause comes about, and then Agent Decem says, "How did you know we were from the other?" My uncle replied snidely, "There isn't too much that I don't know when it comes to you and your organization. Hang tight, based on your PA location, there is an office about five hundred feet to your right, and restrooms in the same area. Help yourself to the food in there. We will be there shortly, and if you haven't noticed, your cell, or sat phones won't work down here, so communication has been cut off from the outside world."

Agent Decem responds, "Understood, and thank you. We will be waiting."

My uncle dials another series of numbers on the PA system. "Anthony, come in."

"Jonathan, this is Jill. Anthony said he was going to go to the tech lab to get something. The supplies are set at the evacuation point. How is everything going down there with James?"

My uncle flags me to come over. "Talk to her." He says. "

Jill, this is James. The training went well, but it's incomplete due to company showing up. How are you doing?"

She says, "Well, under the circumstances fine, and I feel great. Then she whispers, "Thanks for you know what earlier, and I owe you."

I can feel my face get warm, and I glance back at my uncle and Karin, making sure they can't hear.

I say, "Don't worry about it, and umm ... thank you. Are you going to be coming with us to the other facility?"

Jill says, "Yes. All the other preparations have been completed. It looks like there is a good chance that we are going to have to vacate the premises."

I say, "Yeah, it seems that Bentclay is bringing a group of people with him called the Devil...."

Just then I hear my uncle scream out before I could finish, "James!" Jill says, "The Devil King squad. Jonathan how long did you know about this?"

My uncle walks over to the PA, and says, "Edmund left me an encrypted voice message that I was able to listen to about a half an hour ago. It seems that his family was killed by Bentclay's men. He is officially in hiding, so we won't be able to find him unless he wants to contact us."

Jill says, "Oh my God."

"Jill, after this conversation is over I need you to meet up with Anthony on the Red Omega line, and meet us at the Arklay facility. I am going to talk to Anthony now. We will meet in ten minutes."

Jill says, "Jonathan, you need to update James, and Karin on what could possibly happen if the Devil King squad shows up. That was my old unit after all. Okay, then I will see you all there."

My uncle dials another set of numbers on the PA system and says, "Anthony, are you still there?"

Anthony answers, "Yes. I have just retrieved the schematics and all research files saved on the local machines here. I will be sending all the data to our pick up point if things turn south for us. It's Bentclay after all."

My uncle says, "Thanks Anthony. Listen. We are going to rendezvous at the Arklay facility here in the next nine minutes. Take the Omega Red line, and wait for us. Jill is on her way as well."

Anthony says, "Understood, I will see you shortly. Goodbye."

My uncle waves us to follow him. As we begin to follow him I turn to Karin and ask, "What is the Devil King squad? Did Jill work for them?"

Karin says, "I don't know anything about them at all. You'll have to ask your uncle, I guess."

I'm not sure if this is a good time to ask anything at the moment. My uncle tilts his head back and says, "So I guess you want to know what the Devil King squad is, and why Jill sounded slightly upset about the mention of them."

I say, "Yes, please."

"Before, Jill was assigned to spy on me, she was vice captain of the Devil King squad. The Devil King squad doesn't even exist anymore on the books. This was years before Jill's tenure with the squad, but there was an incident about fifteen years ago involving some off-site archeological dig site in Central America that involved reports of the dead walking. The Devil King Squad went in to clean up the mess, but in doing so they killed some innocent civilians, and so for image purposes, they were claimed to have disbanded, and were all supposedly arrested for their crimes. Like I said, they are off the books, and technically don't exist. The reason I know anything about them showing up at all is because of Edmund and his warning to me."

We arrived at the Omega Red line, and got on the shuttle.

My uncle says, "I hope you're ready. From here on out all bets are off, and the day isn't guaranteed. I need you all to stick together. Karin please, if anything happens, and we become separated I am going to need you to continue his training, okay? James, I need you to focus on improving your newly found skills, and work on the technique I showed you earlier. Karin here, take this please."

My uncle hands Karin a flash drive. "This has the training regimen that I had written up just for myself, but now I need you to start it as well. Karin I trust you will help guide his training effectively.

Karin looks shocked, and then says, "Yes, Uncle J, I will."

I know that all of this happening now is for a just in case situation, but now I have a bad feeling, and I just want it to go away. I just found my family again and I don't want anything to happen to them. Somewhere deep down I know that nothing is guaranteed.

BOOP "WELCOME TO THE ARKLAY FACILITY. PLEASE WATCH YOUR STEP." As the door opens out to the lobby I see Anthony, and Jill waiting. Through the looking glass of the door you can see three figures standing in the foyer area. Karin moves over close to me and knocks me forward, as Jill walks towards me and says, "Hey, are you ready?"

I look down for a moment, and say, "Yes, and no. I have no idea what's going to happen, but this is the path I chose, so I must see it through to the end. I have people depending on me now."

She smiles, and my uncle says, "Well, let's go make our introductions; we don't want to keep our guests waiting do we?"

[END CHAPTER SEVENTEEN – INTRODUCTION]

THE JOURNAL PAGES

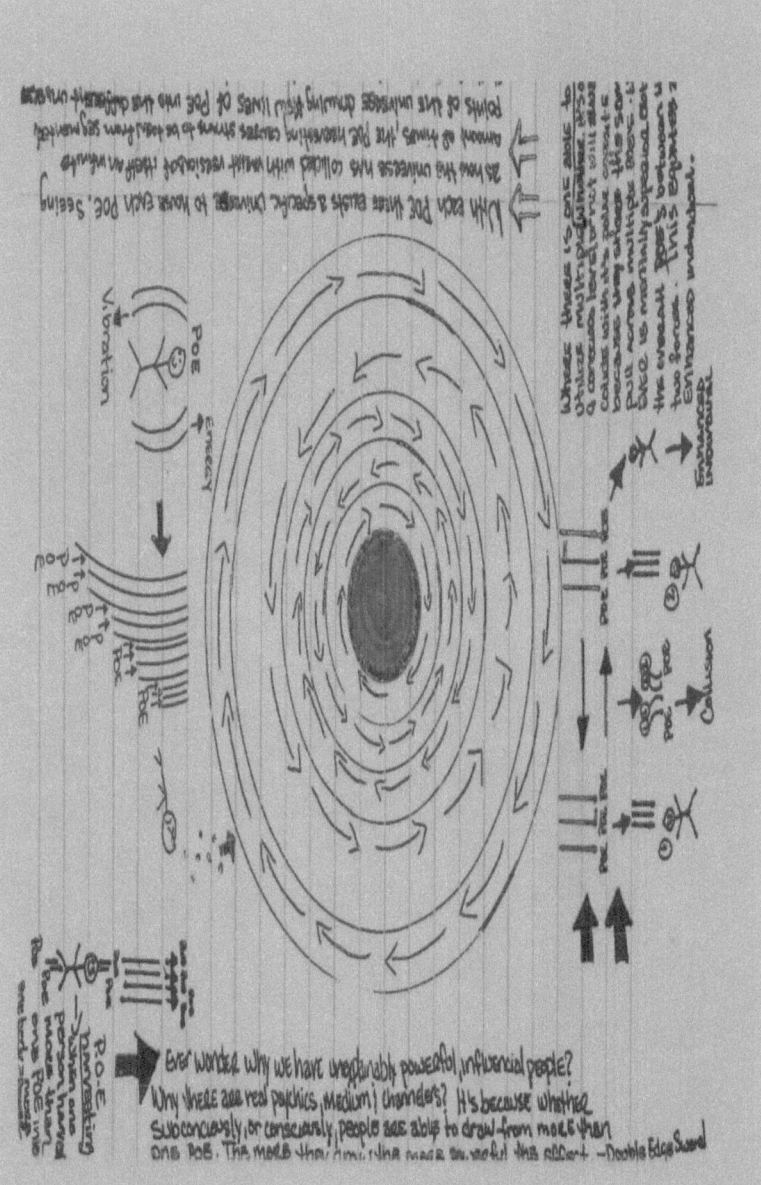

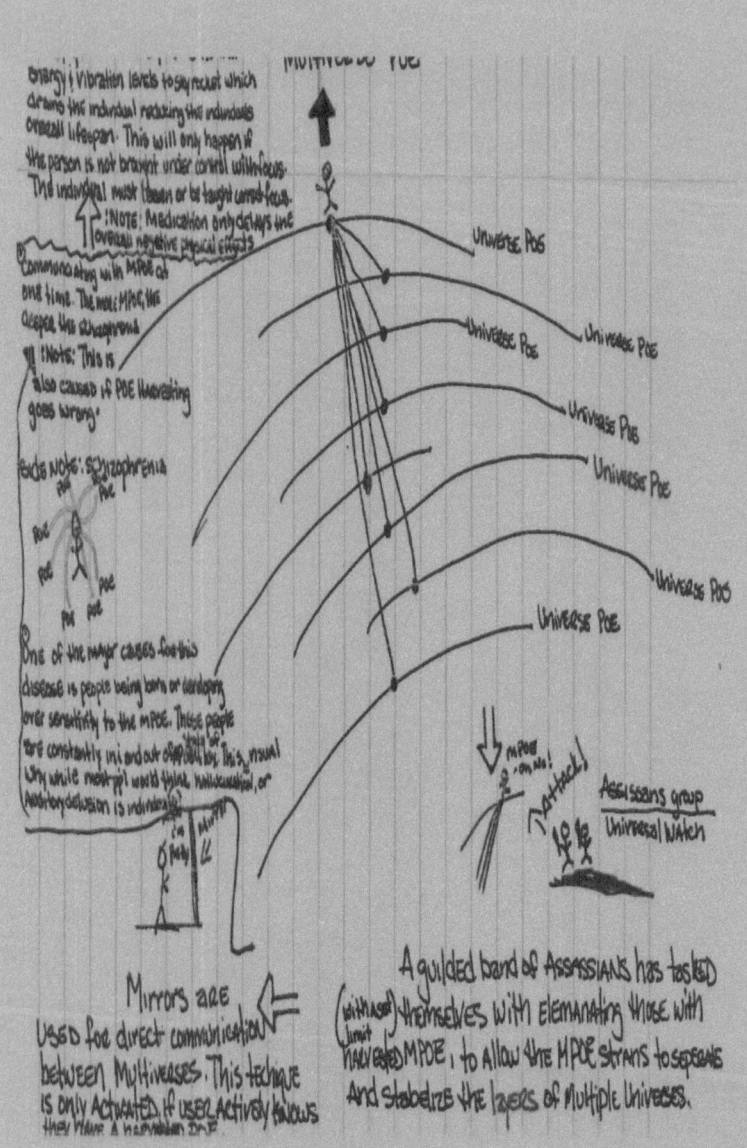

MULTIVERSE POE

energy & vibration levels to say recoil which draws the individual reducing the individuals overall lifespan. This will only happen if the person is not brought under control with focus. The individual must learn or be taught control focus.

:NOTE: Medication only delays the overall negative physical effects

Communicating with MPOE at one time. The more MPOE the deeper the awareness

:Note: This is also caused if POE traveling goes wrong.

Side Note: Schizophrenia

One of the major causes for this disease is people being born or developing over sensitivity to the MPOE. These people are constantly in & out of different Universe's. This visual only while neutral world visual, hallucination, or auditory delusion is individual.

Universe POE
Universe POE
Universe POE
Universe POE
Universe POE
Universe POE
Universe POE
Universe POE

MPOE on me!
Attack!
Assissans group
Universal Watch

Mirrors are used for direct communication between Multiverses. This technique is only Activated if user actively focus they have a heightened POE.

A guilded band of Assassians has tasked (with a set limit) themselves with eleminating those with heightened MPOE, to allow the MPOE strains to seperate and stabelize the layers of multiple universes.

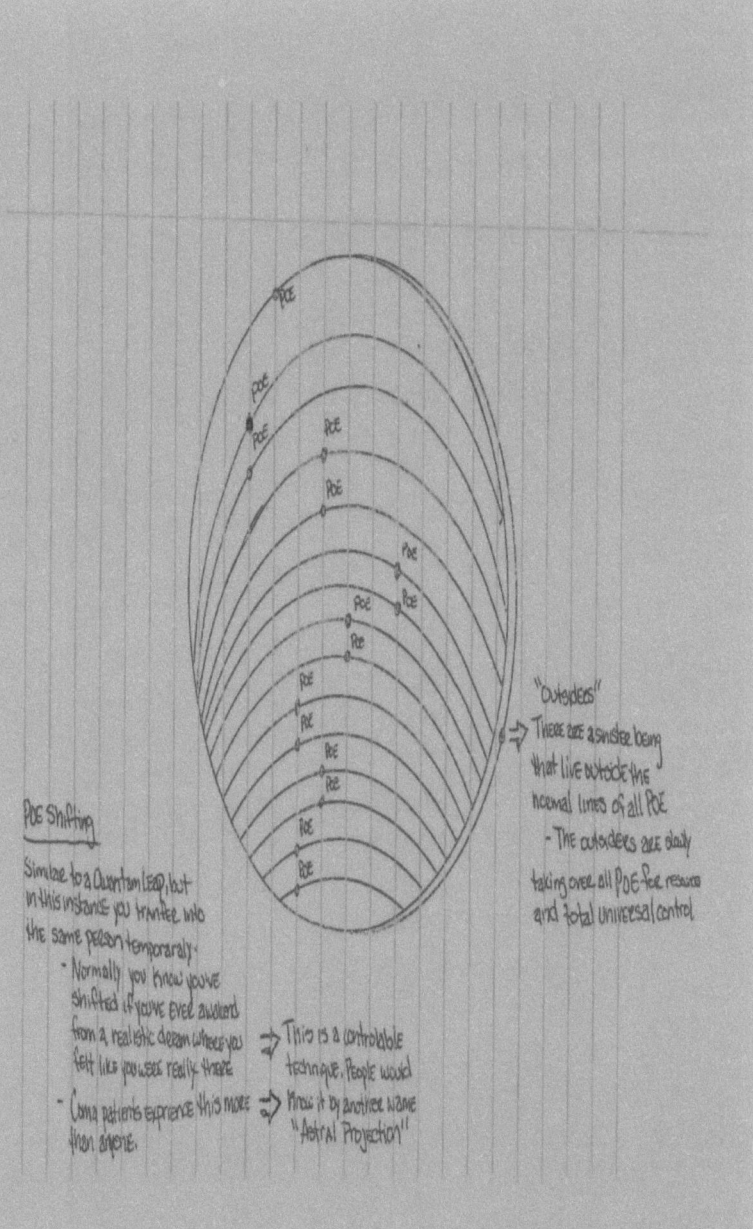

PoE

PoE

PoE

PoE

PoE

PoE

PoE

PoE

PoE

PoE

PoE

PoE

PoE

PoE

PoE

PoE

PoE

"Outsiders"

⇒ There are a sinister being
that live outside the
normal lines of all PoE

  - The outsiders are slowly
taking over all PoE for resource
and total universal control

PoE Shifting

Similar to a Quantum LEAP, but
in this instance you transfer into
the same person temporarily.

  - Normally, you know you've
shifted if you've ever awoken
from a realistic dream where you
felt like you were really there   ⇒ This is a controllable
technique. People would

  - Coma patients experience this more ⇒ Know it by another name
than anyone.   "Astral Projection"

Lines of epiphany - "Also known as Enlightenment"

There are times when the mind is active while "in synch" with the P.O.E minds. As the P.O.E vibrate at different frequencies there are brief times when multiple P.O.E synch in an timed instance.

→ Epiphetic enlightenment

Epiphetic Enlightenment - As multiple P.O.E synchronize for an a timed instance with an active mind (meaning awake) the life lessons from the other P.O.E's all mentally synch. ***NOTE*** synching can be mathmatically timed. Although at the moment the knowing of what P.O.E's synch at specific frequencies can not be calculated.

Within every POE there exsists a LOI.
(Line of intension)

Lines of intension are basically thoughts
of actions that are taken or not taken.
Actions of thought taken or not are all
possible points that all effect our own
POE. Ultimately this affects who we become
in all facets of life.

sample

P.O.E.

LOI

LOI

LOI — President of a successful company — YAY!
life is
good

LOI

LOI

LOI

Poor ; Broke — MAN this
sucks

Decision to endure

Cures all diseases — wow all that
struggle was worth
it

(10) The "Outsiders" uses this (LOI) in order to take
over POE. They have the ability to drive the
individual, convince them to give up all other
POE for certain individual possibilty in an
individuals POE whichs wipes all other
POE into a permanent point of universal
stiching before its actual expressed time of stichin

energy flow
"Energy Absorbed
by "outsiders"

Universal Stiching aka Universal Compression
As An individual's entire POE ends its energy
is returned to its point of origin, but this in
its complete ~Reality~ End.

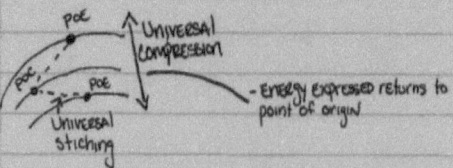

POE
Universal
Compression
POE
POE
- Energy expressed returns to
point of origin
Universal
stiching

(1A) The outsiders have a technique called
POE Universal Stich Coversion. This leads to
All other individual POE expressed energy to
be syphoned outside the Point of Origin (P.O.O)
by the outsiders.

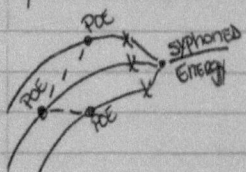

POE
syphoned
Energy
POE
POE

When Coversion occurs the life span of
the particular individual is cut due to
the consistant leak of energy remaining

in the individual. Without the other
POE constant flow of expressed energy
the individual has caused A ~~balance~~
universal unbalance which is corrected
by the point of origin. The remaining
energy is returned & absorbed.

Dominant Transference / Recessive Inclusion
 - Depending on the personality of the
 POE, during the end of one POE, and
 as the energy flows back to the P.O, if
 another POE shares a similar
 existance there is an event called
 P.O.E Unification.

People will dentify these qualities of ~~~~~

- Gamewer
- Ahh man!!

O - Hmmm ... life is great

This allows for an automatic epiphetic enlightenment with attributes of universal which conversion with none of the negative side effects.

POE Unification

POE Unification - During this event as
MPOE are unified ~~there is there~~ there is
an event that allows for traits to layer
within the newly unified POE. In most
instances ~~chosse~~ which ever POE is the more dominant
will retain it's traits in the newly unified
POE, while all previous dominant traits
become recessively included. Which may or
may not affect the overall personality

Indigo Children

— All POE ONE, And
one for all!

These individuals POE are in constant allignment. Although their L.O.I. may differ, but their end path is always the same. Their beginnings & end is stitched together. All experiences are shared simultaneously; And is utilized right away. This leads to very strong effects both mentally & physically. Due to this process the mind of the individual has a virtually limitless ability to access 100% percent of the mind, which allows for the abilities of telepathy, telekenesis, super strength, hearing & sight. Also the ability to commune with oneself accessing the unlimited amount of POE's of itself.

Blink Transfer

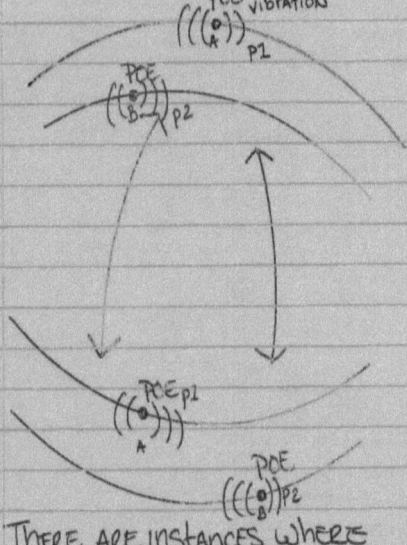

There are instances where,
Two similar POE's energy vibrates
at the same frequency of each other
which cause a shifting between the
individuals POE. The augmented shift
may incur both positive or negative effect

Ex: Driving a vehicle, one moment there is
no vehicle in front; the next minute your in an
accident with a vehicle that wasn't there milliseconds ago

Universe Time Frequency,

Concentric Universe Time ?
Concentric Universal Time Dilation

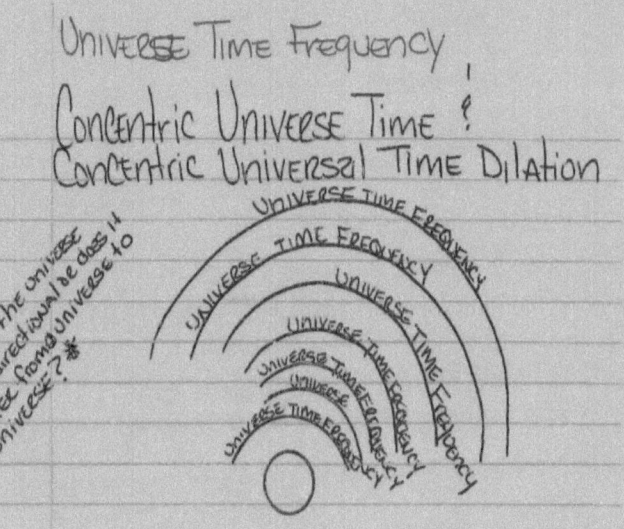

*is the universe unidirectional? de does it differ from a universe to universe? *

While there are multiple Universes they were not all created in the same instance. During the universal expression of the BigBang the universes rippled in creation.

    - This accounts for cases known as DejaVu which effects all individual POE.
This helps to explain the different vibrations of the parallel universes. Its not that they vibrate at different frequencies due to their unique universal fingerprint, but it's due to due to Concentric Universal time dilation

Point of Origin Return

Energy can neither be created nor destroyed. Just as water turns to steam due to environmental conversion, as it cools down it reverts back to its original form. This is the same for the universes created by the Big Bang. As the universes "cool" they collapse & return to the Point of Origin as part of the original universal expression.

When all the expressed energy returns back to the point of origin then the Big Bang happens again

Concentric Universal Time Dilation & Latency Trave Time

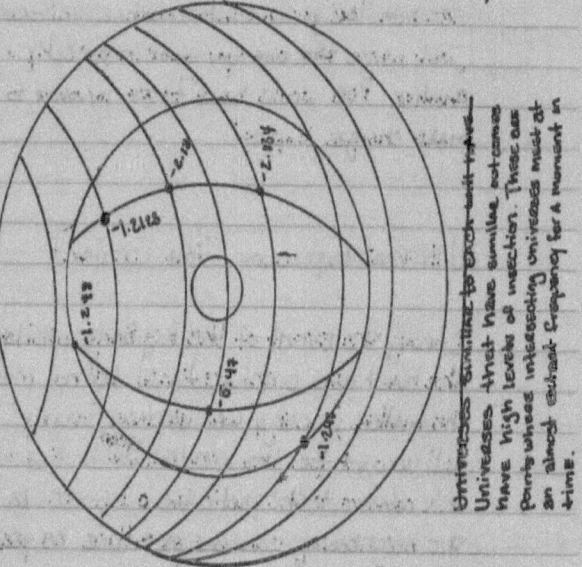

Universes continue to branch until travel. Universes that have similar, outcomes have high levels of injection. These are points where interacting universes meet at an almost extract frequency for a moment in time.

Through every universe CREATED TIME has begun to lapse ;(in every other universe CREATED TIME ITSELF lapses.) NOT sure!! Time itself causes a frequency, ONCE SET that frequency in the universe will not end until time itself ends.'" that universe By understanding and calculating ~~Time Dilations & Latency~~ the Universal Time Frequency you will be able Adjust the Concentric Universal Time Dilation & Latency. With this specific type of calculation you will be able to peer into a probable past or future. Depending if the frequencies are similiar. you can alter another universe just never the one you exist in directly. Another POE would have to be involved to make changes happen.

Universal Expression Time Constant

During the event of the Big Bang, while the blast was omnidirectional does not mean the matter & energy was displaced evenly. This will account for the constant of time being only relative to the particular universe. In short the neighboring universe by either be years ahead of your own civilization, greatly behind, or very much corresponding.

Universal Harmony
Each universe plays out in a certain order governed by LOI. LOI, is governed by the frequency of thought and while no two universes are the same the overall outcomes maybe. When another POE alters the events in another universe, which may disrupt this constant universal flow. One most be careful if treading here.

[??????]

"Tres, Novem, no matter what we stick together. Please allow me to speak to Dr. Edwards solely." Agent Decem says.

As the three agents stand together at the ready in the receiving area, a sense of tension builds, and now, the fate of the agents hangs in the balance. With the knowledge of betrayal and nothing to go back to, Decem, Tres, and Novem leave their past behind walking together into an uncertain future.

[TO BE CONTINUED.......]

www.ingramcontent.com/pod-product-compliance
Lightning Source LLC
Chambersburg PA
CBHW030250200626
46816CB00002BA/579